Michelle Magorian

Be Yourself

EGMONT

This collection first published in Great Britain 2003
by Egmont Books Limited,
239 Kensington High Street, London, W8 6SA

ISBN 1 4052 0272 6

3 5 7 9 10 8 6 4 2

A CIP catalogue record for this title is available from the British Library

Typeset by Avon DataSet Ltd, Bidford on Avon, Warwickshire B50 4JH
Printed and bound in Great Britain by Cox & Wyman Ltd, Reading, Berkshire

Contents

No Sweat

Mark walked out of the men's changing room to the big pool. At the end of the roped-off lanes, under the Charity Swimathon banner, sat men and women with clipboards. Like the attendants they were wearing red Swimathon T-shirts.

Mark stood uncertainly for a moment. He had been told his lane was the second one in from the far side. He walked alongside the pool past the white plastic chairs to where a young man was sitting.

'Are you the lap counter for the twelve to fourteen group?' he asked.

'Yes. Which one are you?'

'Mark. Mark Stevens.'

The man ticked his name. 'Where's the rest of your team?'

'They're coming later. I'm swimming the first hundred lengths and they're sharing the next hundred between them.'

The man nodded.

No sweat, thought Mark.

Mark sat down, his towel draped round his shoulders.

Not that he needed it. It was boiling. He twisted the red bathing-cap they had distributed to all the participants and gazed past the rows of flags, which had been hung above the pool, towards the clock. Nearly two. He dropped his shoulders and blew out a few breaths. Relax, he told himself.

Just then, pop music began blaring out of two speakers. He shaded his eyes with his hands. Even though it was daytime the lights seemed brighter than usual, and there were more of them. He glanced across at the balloons decked out over the boarded-out baby pool. Already people were sitting there at white tables and chairs drinking tea or fruit juice.

To his surprise his stomach was already fluttering. He mustn't get too nervous. Nerves could exhaust you.

He began to take in the teams on either side of his lane. Looking at them through Jacko and Terry's eyes he couldn't help grinning.

On one side was a team of four youths between sixteen and eighteen years old. A short stocky man in his forties wearing a peaked cap was giving them a pep talk, revving them up and waving a stop-watch. Mark guessed they were from a youth club. Boy scout stuff.

He, Jacko and Terry didn't need to join a club. They just got on and did things. No sweat.

Knowing that he was at least four years younger than the team of youths, Mark felt very superior. Just look at them, he thought, hanging on to the coach's every word, looking as serious as if they were entering the Olympics.

The young men began shaking their legs, warming up. Daft that they were all there at the same time, Mark thought. The ones that were third and fourth would be worn out from watching before they had begun.

He glanced at the team on the other side. He couldn't see anyone at first. And then he did.

She was an elderly woman with cropped grey hair. A wrinkly!

He smothered a laugh. He was going to be swimming next to a bunch of wrinklies! He could hear Jacko and Terry's shrieks and feel their powerful elbows crashing into his ribs with mirth.

He looked down hastily. He mustn't get an attack of laughter. He'd never get through one length if he did.

Out of the corner of his eye, he watched her take off a heavy purple towelling robe and pull on her Swimathon bathing-cap. Embarrassing to go around in a swim-suit at her age.

'Attention everyone!' a voice rang out.

Mark sat up straight.

This was it.

A tall man in his fifties was addressing them. Mark knew the rules. He didn't have to hear them. He, Jacko and Terry had studied them enough in the sports centre canteen. No sweat.

Before long, he saw the man approach him.

'On your own?' he asked.

'The rest of my team are coming later.'

'He's doing a hundred,' said Mark's lap counter.

'How old are you?'

'Twelve,' nearly, he added inside his head. 'The others are fourteen.'

The man smiled. 'Good on you.'

To Mark's annoyance he felt a flush of pleasure. He shrugged off the man's remark.

'You'll notice some of the teams will be swimming very fast,' said the man. 'Don't let that bother you. Go at your own pace.'

Mark nodded.

'Hello Joan,' said the man, and he waved at the old woman next to him. 'Back again?'

So the wrinkly's name was Joan. Mark shut his ears to their conversation and looked up at the clock.

He could swim a length a minute up to about thirty lengths and then he'd begin to slow down.

Two hours, he reckoned. Two hours of swimming. Not the best way of thinking about it. He must pace himself, length by length, and keep adding up how much money he could raise for the children's hospital.

Nice to think he'd be earning money by doing something he enjoyed.

'Everyone ready?' said the man in charge.

The coach on his left had his hand on the shoulder of the first youth.

'You can do it,' he was saying firmly.

'Wally,' muttered Mark. He was going to be swimming half the distance Mark was going to swim. Mark pulled on his hat and slipped off his towel.

He heard the wrinkly lower herself into the water. The rest of her team would probably be hobbling in hours later. That is if they hadn't pegged out first.

He was grinning again. Concentrate, he told himself firmly.

He stood up and slipped into the water.

To his surprise, he felt tired. After only one length he was ready to get out. Perhaps breast-stroke was the wrong one to choose. But it was his best stroke. He'd never be able to do the crawl for a hundred lengths.

A high wave from the youth in the next lane sent a gallon of chlorine down Mark's throat and into his eyes. He coughed, gasping for breath. This was a disaster.

Relax, he told himself.

By the third length he'd got his wind back, but he still felt wiped out. He'd steered to the side of the lane, away from the Olympic youth who was crawling at high speed and making waves all around him. The wrinkly was a more sedate swimmer.

It wasn't till he was ten lengths in that the tiredness dissipated. With relief he realised that he had been warming up in the water. That and shaking off his nerves. He had also worked out a steady rhythm. One that he felt would carry him to a hundred.

Now he was enjoying himself. He had started to glide. There was nothing to think about, nothing to worry about. There was just him and the water, the bright lights, the pumping music, the loud splashing and the reverberating voices of the spectators. The noise was deafening.

The first forty lengths were a doddle. It was around his forty-second length when the coach in the next lane started yelling at the youth in the water. 'You can do it! You can do it!'

The three other youths were yelling too, fit to bust. It annoyed Mark, the big deal they were making of it.

Mark couldn't see the youth's head, just a flurry of water drawing closer to the end of the lane. The coach pressed his stop-watch and the next youth lowered himself in. Within seconds, the coach had a towel round the first youth's shoulders and was sending someone off to get hot chocolate like he'd climbed Mount Everest.

Mark turned and pushed off, glancing round for Jacko and Terry. No sign of them yet. Still, there was plenty of time.

It was when the second youth was being urged on to swim faster that the penny dropped. They weren't getting worked up about the number of lengths they were swimming. It was the time they were taking to swim them. They were obviously trying to win some record for speed. That's what all the excitement was about.

As Mark touched the side of the bath, his lap counter

looked up. 'Twelve lengths to go,' he said.

And there was no Jacko and no Terry. They had to arrive soon otherwise Mark's hundred lengths wouldn't even be counted, and his team would be disqualified. Three months of working himself up to a hundred lengths down the tube. And would his sponsors pay up if their team hadn't done the two hundred lengths?

As he turned at the end of the pool, someone put a new tape on. The sound blasted out of the two speakers so loudly it nearly knocked him over.

As Mark headed back towards his lap counter, he realised that part of what had driven him to do a hundred lengths was the desire to impress Jacko and Terry. It was important that they knew he was as tough as them, even though they were approaching six feet and broad-shouldered with it. They had to be there to see him swim that hundred lengths. Be there to show their amazement and slap him on the back even though it stung like a burn when they did it. Then he'd be one of them. They would be a trio, not a duo and a hanger-on. He would never feel lost for words with them again and he'd be able to make jokes as brilliantly as them.

Ninety-eight lengths, two to go.

To his annoyance, he felt a stab of jealousy for the team in the next lane. Not for their swimming ability, he was as good, but because they had mates rooting for every length they swam.

No one was even noticing Mark, aside from the lap counter, who he realised now wasn't allowed to flicker a face muscle.

It was then that he remembered the wrinkly. She was still swimming too. He had been so wrapped up in himself that he hadn't noticed that her team hadn't shown up either.

Mark swam slowly towards the end of the lane. His heart sinking, his fingers touched the wall.

'A hundred,' said the lap counter.

Mark rested his arms over the end.

'What are you going to do?' asked the man.

Mark had a lump in his throat the size of a fist. Do, he thought, do? Cry my bloody eyes out, that's what he felt like doing.

'Sorry, I'm afraid your hundred doesn't count,' he continued.

Mark nodded miserably.

Next to him, the youths were whistling and cheering. If only they'd shut up and the music was turned down, he could think more clearly.

A refined voice pierced through his misery.

It was the wrinkly.

'What's up?' she asked.

None of your business, you old prune, he whispered angrily inside his head.

'His team hasn't turned up.'

'Can't he keep swimming till they do?'

'He's already swum a hundred.'

'I know.' She turned to him. 'I've been watching you out of the corner of my eye. You've done marvellously. Come on, keep going. You can give me moral support.'

'Where's your team?' he asked.

She pointed to herself. 'I'm my team. I'm trying for the two hundred lengths certificate.'

'Two hundred? But that's three miles,' and he stared at her, stunned.

'And a bit.'

'Sorry,' he added quickly, realising his jaw was still open. But he couldn't help himself. A wrinkly going for two hundred lengths!

She laughed.

Mark looked up at his lap counter. 'Can I?'

'Sure, if you think you can manage it.'

'They'll be here soon, I know they will. They've never let me down before. I expect they've been held up somewhere.'

The man nodded.

'Let's go,' said the woman, smiling.

And Mark, in spite of his desire to remain Mr Cool, found himself smiling back.

They pushed themselves on.

Now he really *would* need to pace himself.

He consciously relaxed his shoulders again and pushed more firmly with his legs. No, he thought, his mates had never let him down. Come to think of it, though, he'd never asked them to do anything before. But he hadn't asked them. They'd volunteered. No sweat, they had said. Fifty lengths. Dead easy.

So what had happened to them? He pictured them lying in a pool of blood on Wembley High Street, gasping out some garbled message to the ambulancemen about telling Mark they couldn't make it, but both sinking into unconsciousness before their vital message could be understood.

He touched the wall and turned.

A hundred and one.

Take it easy, he told himself. They'll be here. There's probably been a hold-up on the tube. They were always having trouble on their line. They were probably stuck somewhere, unable to ring the sports centre because the nearest phones had been vandalised. They'd be in a right stew, cursing and pacing the platform and punching walls.

A hundred and two lengths.

He blew heavily into the water. They could be ill of course. Both of them? No. Unless it was food poisoning from a take-away kebab or pizza. Yes, they were probably heaving up somewhere, unable even to keep down a teaspoon of water, struggling to get to the door, picking up their towels, all strength gone, but still determined to make it.

A hundred and three lengths.

When Mark swam his hundred and fiftieth length, he knew that Jacko and Terry weren't going to make it. He turned over on to his back. His neck ached so painfully that he thought it would crack. He'd done a hundred and fifty useless lengths. Useless because in no way could he swim any further. If he could get out and have a break he might make it to two hundred, but it wouldn't count.

He was past caring now. He was so tired he could hardly breathe. He'd take a rest doing a slow back-stroke before climbing out.

Joan was still going. He had to call her Joan now. Wrinkly was the word Jacko and Terry used for anyone elderly and it didn't suit her. He glanced aside at her. She had more guts, stamina and strength than the two of them rolled together. He pictured them making their comments in their trendy jeans and latest trainers and jackets. Legs just that little too far apart, macho men. Hey, Marko, we forgot. He could hear them saying it. No hard feelings, eh? Slam of hand on shoulder. You know how it is? Yeah, thought Mark. I know how it is. Next year, eh? Yeah, next year, or the year after.

He smiled bitterly. His so-called mates had never intended coming at all. Oh yeah, we can do this. Oh yeah, we can do that. No sweat.

And that summed them up. No sweat. They were

incapable of producing a drop of it because they didn't do anything. They were all talk.

Yet he had longed to be one of them. Longed to stop feeling tongue-tied and small and boring. But it wasn't him that was boring. He had just been bored in their company. Bored, bored, bored.

A hundred and fifty-one.

Why hadn't he seen through them before? How come he had believed all their blether? As he lay on his back, a new emotion swept through him. Anger. Anger at them. And anger with himself. As soon as he touched the wall he turned over and began to crawl. He still knew he wouldn't make it, but at least moving his neck from side to side would ease the pain. He lashed out furiously into the water like a tiger released from captivity. Wild and powerful, yet still in control. Still graceful.

As he crawled length after length he swam out all the feelings he had kept bottled up inside him for months. All the doubts he had ignored when Jacko and Terry never turned up for a practise with him, but told him they were practising on other days. How could he have been so stupid? Because he was desperate to have friends. Any friends.

Almost the dullest in his class, but not quite. Never feeling he could mix with the dumbos or the ones that got by. Switched off and switched out. That was him.

A hundred and seventy lengths.

The team beside him had finished. They were jubilant. Well-pleased with themselves.

Joan was still swimming. As if she sensed him looking at her she beamed at him. 'Think I'll make it?' she yelled.

'Yeah, 'course you will.' He nearly said, 'no sweat,' but stopped himself.

His neck had eased up now. His shoulders and ankles ached instead. He rolled over into the back-stroke again to give himself another rest.

By the time Mark completed his one hundred and eightieth length, there was no one left in the pool except him and Joan. The only people around the pool were their two lap counters and a life-guard on a high-seated podium at the side.

The man who was in charge came out of the office and gazed in Mark's direction.

Don't say he's going to disqualify me now, thought Mark. But the man grinned and raised two thumbs. He was rooting for him! He gave Joan the same message.

It was then that Mark noticed that the life-guard was smiling. Mark hadn't even bothered to look at him. And he gave a thumbs-up sign too! Three people wanted him to make it. It pushed him to complete the next length.

Soon after this incident, attendants came out of the office, curious to watch Joan and him. They appeared relaxed and not at all bothered at having to stay behind.

The early evening sun had found its way to a long window at the side and it streamed into the pool. Someone had turned the music off. It was so quiet that Mark could hear the water lapping around him. He could have been swimming in a private pool in Malibu.

Two attendants were removing the flags above their heads.

'Take your time,' said his lap counter, picking up Mark's anxiety. 'Keep to your own steady pace, we're not in a hurry.'

Ten lengths to go and he knew. He knew he was going to make it.

Please don't let me pass out, get cramp or die, he told himself.

Attendants had begun to gather round his lap counter who was now fighting down a smile.

'Come on, you're nearly there,' shouted a tall blonde-haired girl.

Mark nearly choked. Jacko and Terry had been lusting after her for weeks. They never said hello to her of course. They just stared at her and talked about her. And here she was rooting for him, twelve years old, nearly, and puny. Correction, he told himself. Puny people don't swim a hundred and ninety-two lengths. Three miles!

He laughed. He had no friends and he was laughing. Crazy. But he decided he'd rather be himself and have no friends than try and pretend to be someone he wasn't. And it made him feel feather-light.

14

It was the last length and it was so sweet he didn't want to rush it. Joan knew and she cheered from the water. And then everyone round the pool was clapping. And the man in charge was clasping his hands above his head.

Mark came in on a leisured crawl, touched the side and hung there, high. He swam to the steps at the side. He was too weak to pull himself out of the pool from the water. He had hardly reached the chairs when his legs buckled. He sat down quickly and wrapped the towel around his aching shoulders. His legs were shaking. His ankles ached and his feet felt as though someone had stuck them in a fridge. All he wanted to do was collapse into bed and sleep.

'Two hundred lengths,' said his lap counter, smiling.

Mark nodded, still trying to catch his breath. The man in charge grinned down at him.

'Looks like you didn't need your team-mates after all.'

'Yeah,' he agreed.

The man handed him an orange juice. Mark held it for a moment and then sipped it slowly. He wanted to sit still and take in what he had achieved: 'Two hundred lengths,' he whispered. 'I have just swum two hundred lengths.' He had proved something to himself. He wasn't sure what, but it felt very good.

'You'd best get dressed before you get too cold,' said the lap counter.

'Not yet,' said Mark, putting down the beaker.

'It's over now.'

'Not for Joan it isn't.' And he pulled himself shakily to his feet, stumbled over to her lane, and started yelling.

The Greatest

'Boys group,' said the teacher.

The second group of girls broke away from the centre of the dance studio, their faces flushed, their skin streaming with sweat.

A skinny girl, whose fair hair was scraped up into a bun, smiled at him, and pretended to collapse with exhaustion against the barre.

'Kevin, aren't you a boy any more?' asked the teacher.

'Oh yes,' he exclaimed. 'Sorry.'

He joined the other three boys in the class. They were waiting for him opposite the mirror.

'You've been in a dream today,' she said. 'Now I expect some nice high jumps from you boys, so we'll take it slower. That doesn't mean flat feet. I want to see those feet stretched. First position. And one and two.'

Kevin brought his arms up into first in front of him and out to the side to prepare for the jumps.

He loved the music the pianist chose for them. It made him feel as if he could leap as high and as powerfully as Mikhail Barishnikov. He knew that barre work was important but he liked the exercises in the centre of the studio best, especially when they had to leap.

But today all the spring had gone out of him. A lead weight seemed to pull him down. Bending his knees in a deep *pliè* he thrust himself as high as he could into the air.

'I want to see the effort in your legs, not your faces,' remarked the teacher as he was in mid-spring.

They sprang in first position, their feet together, and out into second with their feet apart, then alternated from one to the other, out in, out in, sixteen times in each position, sixteen times for the change-overs.

'Don't collapse when you've finished,' said the teacher. 'Head up. Tummies in. And hold. Right everyone, back into the centre.'

It was the end of class. The girls made wide sweeping curtsies, the boys stepped to each side with the music and bowed.

'Thank you,' said the teacher.

They clapped to show their appreciation, as if they were in an adult class. Kevin knew that was what they did because in the holidays he was sometimes allowed to attend their Beginners' Classes in Ballet, even though he was only ten. He was more advanced than a beginner but at least the classes kept him fit.

Everyone ran to the corner of the studio to pick up their bags. It wasn't wise to leave any belongings in the changing rooms. Too many things had been stolen from there.

The teacher stood by the door taking money from those who paid per class, or tickets from those whose parents paid for them ten at a time, which was cheaper.

Martin was standing in front of him, pouring out a handful of loose change into the teacher's tin. His father disapproved of boys or men doing ballet, so Martin did it in secret and paid for his classes and fares by doing odd jobs. His only pair of dance tights were in ribbons and his dance shoes were so small that they hurt him.

Kevin handed his ticket to the teacher.

'I saw your father earlier on,' she said. 'Whose class is he taking?'

'He's not doing a class. It's an audition.'

'Is that why your head is full of cotton wool today? Worried for him?'

'Not exactly,' he said slowly.

He tugged at Martin's damp T-shirt.

'Dad gave me extra money today. I have to wait for him. Want some orange juice?'

'Yeah,' said Martin eagerly.

'Let's grab a table.'

They ran down the corridor to the canteen area and flung their bags on to chairs.

'I'm bushed,' said Martin.

'Were you sweeping up Mr Grotowsky's shop this morning?'

'Yeah. And I cleaned cars. Dad thinks I'm working this afternoon, too.'

'What if he checks up?'

'He won't. As long as he doesn't see me he doesn't care where I am.'

'Doesn't he wonder why you don't have any money when you go home?'

'No. I tell him I spend it on Wimpy's or fruit machines.'

Although he was only eleven, Martin had already decided what he wanted to do with his life. He had it all mapped out. First he'd be a dancer, then a choreographer. His idol was a tall thin black American teacher in the Big Studio. He had performed in and choreographed shows in the West End. Professional dancers and students sweated and slaved for him, arching and stretching, moving in fast rhythms, leaping and spinning. There were black ones there too, like Martin. One day one of those black dancers would be him.

Some of the students were afraid of the teacher but they worked hard to be allowed to get into, and stay in, his classes.

'Get a classical training first,' he had told Martin abruptly when Martin had plucked up enough courage to ask his advice. So that's what Martin was doing.

'What's the audition for?' he asked.

'A musical.'

Kevin put their beakers of orange on to the table.

'So what's the problem? Don't you think he has a chance?'

Kevin shrugged.

'Which one is it?'

'*Guys and Dolls*. He's going up for an acting part. He thinks his best chance of getting work as an actor is if he gets into a musical. He says no one will look at him if they know he's a dancer. He says directors think dancers haven't any brains.'

'I'd like to see them try a class.'

'Yes. That's what Dad says.'

'Is it because you're nervous for him? Is that it?'

'No. We had a row this morning. We just ended up shouting at one another. We didn't talk to each other all the way here. Even in the changing room.'

'What was the row about?'

'About him auditioning for this job. I don't want him to get it.'

'Why? He's been going to enough voice classes.'

'Yes, I know,' he mumbled.

For the last year, his father had been doing voice exercises every morning, taking singing lessons, working on scenes from plays at the Actors' Centre, practising audition speeches and songs, and reading plays.

'I didn't think he'd have to go away though. This theatre's a repertory theatre and it's miles away. I'd only see him at the weekend. And even then it'd probably only be Sundays. And if he got it he'd start rehearsing two weeks after I start school.'

'So? You've been there before. Not like me. I start at the

Comprehensive in a week's time. It'll be back to Saturday classes only.' He swallowed the last dregs of his orange juice.

'Want another? Dad said it was OK.'

'Yeah. I'll go and get them.'

Kevin handed him the money and pulled on his tracksuit top over his T-shirt even though he was still boiling from the class.

He couldn't imagine his father being an actor. But his father had explained that he couldn't be a dancer all his life, that choreographers would eventually turn him down for younger dancers and, in fact, had already done so a couple of times. He had to decide which direction he wanted to go in before that started to become a habit.

For the last two years, since Kevin's mother had died, his father had only accepted work in cabaret in London, or bit parts in films, or had given dance classes. Otherwise he had been on the dole. Kevin was used to him being around now.

When his mother was alive and his parents were touring with a dance company, Kevin used to stay with a friend of the family. Dad said it would be like old times staying with her again. Kevin didn't want it to be like old times. He wanted things to stay just as they were.

He pulled on his tracksuit trousers, dumped his holdall on his chair and waved to Martin.

'I'll be back in a minute,' he yelled.

He ran down the two flights of stairs which led to the entrance hall, past two of the studios there and downstairs to the basement where the changing rooms and other studios were.

Outside the studio where the audition was taking place stood a crowd of people peering in at the windows. They were blocking the corridor so that dancers going to and from the changing room had to keep pushing their way through with an urgent 'Excuse me!'

The door to the studio opened and six disappointed men came out. Kevin's father wasn't among them.

Kevin squeezed in between two people by one of the windows and peered in.

Inside the steamed-up studio, a group of men of every age, height and shape were listening to a woman director. A man was sitting at a piano.

The director was smiling and waving her arms about.

'Here. Squeeze in here,' said a dancer in a red leotard. 'You can see better. They're auditioning for *Guys and Dolls*. It's the men's turn today.'

Kevin didn't let on that he knew.

'She's really putting them through it,' said the dancer. 'First they have to sing on their own and the MD, that's the man at the piano, decides who's going to stay. Then they have to learn a song together.'

'What's the song?' asked Kevin.

'"Luck Be a Lady Tonight". Know it?'

Kevin nodded.

Know it? As soon as his father had heard he had been

given the audition, every song from *Guys and Dolls* had been played from breakfast to bedtime.

'Then they have to do an improvisation. The director chooses who to keep out of that lot and then the choreographer teaches them a dance routine.'

The dancing would be kid's stuff for his father, thought Kevin. He wiped the glass. His father was standing listening. So, he'd passed two singing tests. Now it was the acting.

The director was obviously explaining what the scene was about. She was pointing to individual men.

'She's telling them about the characters,' said the dancer.

Kevin felt angry. How could his father go through with it when he knew that Kevin didn't want him to go away? He observed his father's face, watched him grip his arms in front of himself and then quickly drop them and let out a breath.

'Excuse me!' he said fiercely, and he pushed himself out of the crowd and along the corridor to the stairs. And then he stopped. He remembered the look on his father's face and realised it was one of anxiety. It astounded him. He had seen his father upset before, but never scared. Why would he be scared? He was a brilliant dancer. But now, of course, he also needed to be a good actor. He was trying something new in front of actors who had been doing it for years and some of those actors were younger than him. That took guts, as Martin would say.

Kevin hadn't given a thought to how nervous his father

might have been feeling. He knew how badly he missed the theatre. To start a new career when you were as old as him must be hard; harder too when he knew that Kevin hoped he would fail.

He turned and ran back down the corridor, ducked his head and pushed his way back into the crowd to where the dancer in the red leotard was standing. He wasn't too late. They hadn't started the improvisation yet. He stared through the glass willing his father to look at him.

The director stopped talking. The men began to move, their heads down in concentration as she backed away.

Please look this way, thought Kevin.

And then he did. He frowned and gazed sadly at him.

Kevin raised his thumb and mouthed, 'Good luck!'

At that, his father's face burst into a smile.

'Thanks,' he mouthed back and he winked.

Kevin gave a wave and backed away through the crowd and along the corridor.

It was going to be all right, he thought. If his father did get the acting job, he knew he'd be taken backstage and he'd meet lots of new people, and at least he wouldn't be touring so he could stay with him sometimes. And Martin could come too. And Dad would be happy again.

Martin wasn't at the table. Their bags were still there with the two plastic beakers of orange juice. Kevin knew where to find him. He walked to the corridor. Martin was gazing with admiration through one of the windows into the Big Studio. His idol was giving a class to the professional dancers.

He grinned when he saw Kevin.

'Guess what!' he squeaked. 'I was by the door when he went in and he noticed me. And he spoke to me. He looked at my shoes and he said I ought to swap them for bigger ones at Lost Property and then, you know what he said? He said, "Say I sent you!"'

He turned back to watching the class and sighed.

'Isn't he the greatest?'

'Yes,' agreed Kevin, and he thought of his father. 'Yes, he's the greatest.'

Sea Legs

1

Tessa was flung violently against the side of the deep cockpit. Blinded by her fringe, she clung fiercely to the coaming with one hand and dragged her long brown hair from her eyes and mouth with the other. She had just managed to shove a tangled clump of it into her shirt, when a wave swept over the deck and broke against the doghouse. Before she could duck, a deluge of cold foam tumbled into the cockpit and streamed down the steps into the cabin.

She slid down and crouched, her face dripping, her baggy cotton sweater and trousers billowing damply around her. She had never expected the sea to be this rough, this cold or this terrifying.

She dragged herself up to the left side of the cockpit and thought wryly of the contents of her holdall, now thrown across the cabin. Inside it were textbooks and her swim-suit. She had planned to spend some time sunbathing before going below to do her homework. She had even imagined herself on deck waving to people in their colourful yachts as they glided alongside them in the sunlight. What a joke!

Suddenly the sodden mainsail above her head started to flap wildly and the next thing she knew she was being pushed firmly but gently aside. It was Joseph. He had sprung upwards towards her after casting off one rope and was frantically hauling in another. They were changing tack.

Tessa pinned herself against the back of the cockpit and stared up mesmerised.

'Boom coming over!' yelled Joseph to his friend at the helm. Like a fool, Tessa, who was miles out of reach, dropped quickly on to her heels as a thick piece of timber the size of a telegraph-pole arced over them. The boat lurched and she crashed to the floor hitting an elbow. By the time she had clawed herself up, the boat was tipped so far on the other side that the sails were being pulled through the water.

Acutely aware that she was wearing no life-jacket or harness, Tessa wondered whether she would ever see her parents again. I want this to be over, she prayed, and soon.

It had seemed years since she had left Rye with her Uncle Nick and his two bachelor friends in the yacht. 'Yacht' was what her uncle had called it when chatting enthusiastically to anyone he could strike up a conversation about it with.

When he had taken her down to the moorings after lunch, she was stunned to find that it bore no resemblance to the glossy blue and white vessel she had imagined. Instead it was a sixty year old wooden cutter, with peeling paint around her white hull.

Below decks, inside the cabin, four old bunks were held up by chains. Standing solidly between them, to the front of the cabin, was the lower section of the huge wooden mast. As she stepped down she spotted a tatty two-burner stove on her left. Above the working surface beside it, plates were held in place by wooden batons near a row of stained mugs on hooks. To her right was a large dark varnished box, which she later discovered housed the engine. A chart was laid out on it.

She quickly realised that the chart table would be the only place she could do any of her weekend homework. There was no other furniture; no curtains by the three oval portholes on either side of the top bunks, and no carpets.

Tossed on to the wooden floor were ropes tied up in long loops and from the beams across the roof hung a couple of blackened oil-lamps.

Staring into the tacky gloom she had been speechless with disappointment. At least she could console herself with the thought that she wouldn't be spending the night in it. She could look forward to staying up late and getting spoiled by her uncle when they returned to his house.

The second surprise of the day was discovering that the cutter was owned by three men. Her family had always been given the impression that her uncle owned it outright and took a crew with him. The other two owners were friends, Joseph and Ted.

Joseph was hauling up the mainsail when they arrived, and Ted was twiddling a knob on a small transistor which was perched on a shelf under the doghouse.

She could tell by their faces they were surprised to see her.

Her uncle had hardly begun to talk nautical gobblede-gook to her about jibs and staysails when Ted whirled round and snapped out, 'Shut up!'

To her amazement her uncle obeyed.

'Why should he?' she muttered crossly.

'Quiet!' he yelled.

'Is that how your crew speak to you?' she exclaimed.

'Shhh!' added Joseph, who was now leaning over the doghouse listening intently.

It was only then that she realised they were trying to listen to the weather forecast and had missed the essential bit because she and her uncle had been talking at the crucial moment. It didn't make for a great introduction.

Embarrassed, Tessa had sat hunched on the deck with her legs dangling into the cockpit. Luckily her uncle's friends were too busy preparing to sail to take much notice of her, so she took advantage of her invisible state to give them the once over.

Joseph was slim and wiry and always on the move, hauling or tying up ropes (though she discovered fairly quickly that the ropes attached to the sails were referred to as sheets). He sprang rather than walked, and when he spoke, it was excitedly and at a rapid rate. His blond hair and beard were bleached and tangled from sun and salt spray and his face was such a brick-red colour that his crooked teeth showed up white against his sunburnt mouth.

Ted was tanned too, but brown. He was quiet with dark hair and vibrant green eyes. Tessa had the impression that he didn't suffer fools gladly. She suspected he didn't like children either. When her uncle asked if anyone minded him bringing along his twelve-year-old niece, she had heard Ted mutter, 'It's a bit late to ask us if we mind now,' and later, 'This is not a crèche!'

Her uncle called out to her. He was untying the old car tyres they used as fenders. He handed them to her to chuck down on to the cabin floor.

'We have to move fast,' he explained. 'We only have an hour around high tide to get over the harbour bar and out into the sea.'

She had smiled up at him. He looked so nautical with his salt and pepper beard, his navy cap, stripy T-shirt and white trousers. At least he was dressed for sailing, not like Joseph and Ted. They were actually wearing jumpers even though the sun was beating down on them. She had assumed it was because, being middle-aged, they felt the cold more.

Later she was to envy them those jumpers.

But then, sitting beside her uncle in the front, motoring

happily down the river, protected by the mud-flats, their sails set ready for the open sea, she had felt as though she was about to embark on a great adventure. Warmed by the sun, accompanied only by the sounds of the chugging of the engine down below and seagulls, she brushed aside the awfulness of the boat itself and returned to thinking about her homework. As long as she could get at least half of it done it would be a successful afternoon. How could she have foreseen that as soon as the boat hit the open sea her uncle would be struck down by a mysterious illness and disappear into one of the bottom bunks where he would lie motionless, only to lift his head occasionally to commune with a large black bucket beside him; that she would be left alone with two men she didn't know – one of whom would have preferred her to have remained on shore – in a creaky old boat in gale-force winds. And if that wasn't enough, within half an hour of leaving Rye, she had been bursting for a pee but had been too embarrassed to ask for the loo. She knew there was one on board somewhere. Her uncle had mentioned it to her vaguely, only he had called it the 'Heads'.

She turned to speak to Joseph, but was shocked to discover he had gone. Terrified, she forced herself to cross over to the other side of the cockpit. Ted was perched high on the back of it hanging on to the tiller and staring sullenly out to the sea. Avoiding him, she made a leap for the coaming, missed, and slid backwards on her hands and knees. She struggled to her feet and was about to fall again when he caught her by the collar, pulled her towards him and flung her on to one of the wooden steps below him.

'Thanks,' she gasped.

'What are you trying to do?' he yelled.

'See Joseph. Where is he?'

'On deck. Reefing,' answered Ted curtly.

The wind whistled and roared into her aching ears.

'Weeping?' she said, alarmed.

'Reefing,' he snapped. 'It means he's going to take in the sails a bit. Make them smaller, so that there's less power in them and we have more control of the boat.'

When he looked up sharply at the small flag at the top of the mast she gathered he didn't wish to speak any further.

She climbed up on to the step, pinned her arms over the coaming and peered out.

One of the front sails had been taken down, the staysail. The mainsail had been dropped halfway down the mast. Joseph was pulling it towards him in armfuls, rolling it and lacing it down to the boom. Each time the boat pitched, Tessa had to shove her knuckles into her mouth to prevent herself from screaming, for it looked as if he were about to be flung over the little rail that surrounded the boat and out into the sea. As he edged himself further along the boom and nearer the cockpit she willed him to survive. Joseph was her only hope. There was no way she could ask Ted where the toilets were.

As soon as he had thrown himself into the cockpit she felt safer. She took a deep breath but before she could open her mouth, he and Ted began a discussion about beating against a south-westerly wind.

'We'll just have to keep heading for Newhaven,' she heard Joseph yelling up to Ted.

'In this?' he cried. 'It could take till tomorrow.'

'Tomorrow!' shrieked Tessa, but her voice was smothered by the wind.

'There's no point returning,' shouted Joseph. 'We'd have to sail up and down this bay for about twelve hours waiting for high tide again. If we head for Newhaven at least we'll be going somewhere.'

Ted gave a nod and Joseph leapt down the steps in to the cabin. Tessa made a wild dash to the doorway and stumbled in after him.

'Joseph!' she yelled.

He was examining a chart on the lid of the engine-box. She touched his shoulder. He turned and smiled.

'Are we really not going back to Rye?' she asked anxiously.

'No. It would be too ignominious.'

'What does that mean?'

'Embarrassing. And it'd be too dangerous. The entrance to Rye is pretty choppy in bad weather. You should see how steep the waves get. Bigger boats than ours, even ones with powerful engines, have been wrecked there.'

He returned to the chart.

'Joseph,' she began. 'I was wondering . . .'

'What I'm doing?' he asked.

'Sort of. But first . . .' She hesitated.

It was in that moment of hesitation that they heard a loud rattling sound, like an underground train roaring underneath them.

'Good God!' cried Joseph, pushing her aside. 'What on earth's that?'

Tessa stayed on the top step and clung to the doorway paralysed with terror. She remembered having heard of submarines wrecking fishing boats. Any minute she expected the boat to be shattered into pieces underneath them. The two men, their faces alert, were scrutinising everything in sight.

Suddenly Joseph gave a violent start.

'It's the chain,' he screamed, and he leapt out of sight.

Ted peered out towards the front of the boat alarmed, while the monstrous rattling sound continued to thunder beneath them. Imagining what was going on was too terrifying for Tessa. She threw herself against the coaming and craned her neck over it to see what was happening. It was then that she saw what was making the noise. Rattling at breakneck speed over the side of the boat was a large iron chain. Joseph was trying to stop it, but it was moving at such speed that it nearly took him with it. Tessa watched, riveted with fear, as he attempted to step on it with his foot, but it was useless. The chain continued to pour out.

'Ted, what's happening?'

She could see he was worried.

'The anchor's gone over the side.'

Joseph was sprinting along the deck towards them.

'If we don't stop the boat, the chain'll rip the deck out!' he hollered. 'Start the engine! Full astern! Put her head into the wind!'

'Take the tiller!' commanded Ted. 'And keep it steady.'

She jumped up on to the step, and grabbed it.

Ted was on his knees pulling at a small lever. The engine gave a low throttling sound.

The boat gave a lurch. Tessa gripped the tiller till she ached. It seemed that it was all that was between her and a watery death.

The next thing she knew, she was buried in heavy wet canvas. She struggled to keep her legs braced on the step.

'Get the bloody sail off me!' she heard Ted yelling.

'I'm pulling it off as fast as I can,' came Joseph's voice through the wind.

'Are we going to drown?' Tessa whimpered.

'Not if I can help it,' grunted Ted from somewhere. 'Just stay put.'

Stay put! Where else could she go?

The boat pitched violently again.

Soaked and shaking Tessa felt the heavy canvas being pulled across her.

She hooked one arm firmly over the helm and shoved up

a wedge of the sail with her free arm. But it was still too heavy for her to budge.

'Stop the engine!' she heard Joseph roar. 'It's useless in this sea. We're just turning in circles round the anchor.'

The engine spluttered to a halt.

'What's happened?' shouted Ted.

'We're in luck. The deck's intact. The bitter end hasn't come out.'

She heard Ted give a cry of relief.

Just then there was a clattering noise from below.

'Ted!' a voice called out.

It was her uncle.

'What?'

'Are we in Newhaven?'

Tessa heard a strangled, outraged snort.

'No!' Ted yelled. 'And we probably won't be there until tomorrow.'

There was a brief silence broken eventually by the muffled sounds of vomiting.

There was no need for him to be that harsh with her uncle, thought Tessa angrily. He was a sick man. How was he to know he would get food poisoning, or some virus, as soon as they left Rye?

She was about to come to his defence when she noticed that the canvas was no longer crushing her. She gave it a shove and managed to stick her head out. She gulped in the bitter wind, her hair rising up and round her head like a gorgon's. Joseph was hauling armfuls of mainsail up and shoving it round the boom. There was mainsail everywhere. It filled the cockpit, overflowed on to the deck and trailed into the sea.

From her high position she saw that the jib had been yanked down.

The canvas below her began to move. It was Ted fighting his way out. He pulled aside the sail and within seconds was heading towards the jib, clinging on to parts of the boat as he staggered towards the small trailing sail.

She watched him throw back a trapdoor, remove the jib, and sling it below. It was only then that she realised where the lavatory must be.

'So near, yet so far,' she murmured.

Ted joined Joseph and within minutes she felt the canvas being lifted from her shoulders.

The two men tied the remainder of the sail to the boom and half-jumped, half-fell into the cockpit talking rapidly in their nautical gibberish.

'I'll just have to sweat it up by hand,' Joseph was saying.

Ted clambered up on to the step and relieved Tessa of the tiller, not that it was doing anything. Tessa slid gratefully on to the step and leaned back.

Suddenly they stopped talking and she found that they were staring at her. She grinned up at them, her teeth chattering.

'Is that all the clothing you have?' inquired Joseph.

'Yes. But it's OK. I'm fine,' she said, shrugging it off bravely.

'I've a spare pair of socks, jeans and Guernsey on the bottom bunk,' he said. 'Put them on and grab some waterproofs and a hat from the pegs by the door behind the mast.'

'I'll be all right,' she said jovially, feeling like death.

'Don't be a martyr,' snapped Ted. 'We can't afford to have two sick people on board.'

'It's important to stay warm,' added Joseph gently. 'We don't want you getting hypothermia.'

'But only old ladies get that,' she protested.

'Don't you believe it. Anyone can get it out at sea.'

'OK,' she mumbled, and she reeled towards the cabin.

Suddenly she whirled round, 'Joseph,' she said puzzled. 'What's a Guernsey?'

2

Down in the dark cabin, she glanced quickly at her sleeping uncle and back up to the cockpit. Ted and Joseph were still busy talking. Convinced that no one was watching, she hastily peeled off her sodden trousers and socks and pulled on Joseph's. She folded the waistband of his jeans over and made large turn-ups before lacing up her canvas shoes. The Guernsey was an old navy-blue jumper with stitching at the top of the sleeves just under the shoulders. She dragged off her soaked sweater and put it on. The warmth was immediate. With the cuffs rolled back she almost felt comfortable.

The boat gave another lurch flinging her against the mast. She hugged it and slid her way round to where the waterproofs were hanging. She had hardly let go when she was thrown against a door. Realising it must be the door to the Heads, she turned the bronze handle. Nothing happened. In desperation she jammed her shoulder hard against it and gave a hefty push. It only budged slightly. And then she remembered the sails. They were obviously blocking the door. If she hadn't begun to feel queasy she could easily have howled with rage. She grabbed some yellow oilskins and an old tweed cap and scrambled back to the cockpit.

Feeling nauseous she hung her head over the coaming. The cold air buffeted and roared round her but it was heaven compared to the sick-making cabin. She began to hum rapidly. It was her cure for coach-sickness. She was praying it would have the same effect on a boat. As soon as the wind began to toss her hair about again, she stuck the cap on and tucked any loose strands behind her ears. Still staring with fixed concentration at the sea she breathed in deeply and pulled on the oilskin jacket. Ted yelled at her.

She swung round alarmed.

'You put the trousers on underneath,' he explained. 'They'll cover your chest.'

Tessa could feel her face growing scarlet. As soon as she had spotted the braces she knew she had to put the trousers on first, but she wanted to wait until she had been to the Heads.

'I'll do it later,' she stammered, and turned hurriedly away to see what Joseph was doing.

He was sitting on the foredeck, his feet straddled against the toe-rail, hauling up the heavy wet chain and tossing it into a heap behind him. With each convulsive heave of his body he gave a loud grunt. It was obvious he was using every ounce of his strength.

There was no way she could ask him to help her now. She hung vehemently to the coaming as the boat continued to be pitched about. Her stomach ached from controlling herself for so long, and every time the boat lurched, the pain made her feel sicker. She realised she would have to swallow her embarrassment and ask Ted.

When she looked up at him she found he was peering through a pair of binoculars. His expression was grim.

'Ted!' she yelled.

He glared down at her. 'How long do you think Joseph will be?' she asked nonchalantly.

He shrugged. 'There's sixty fathoms of chain. In these conditions it could take an hour. Could take three hours. Why?'

Against her will she heard herself saying, 'Just wondering when he'd like a cup of tea, that's all.'

For a fraction of a second she actually detected a slight smile.

'Later,' he said.

Miserable, she returned to staring at the sea.

'Idiot!' she muttered angrily to herself, and she pressed her forehead hard against her knuckles.

An hour later Joseph was still dragging up the chain on to the deck from his semi-crouched position. She watched him as he shoved each glistening pile of chain down a small hole in the deck before hauling the next lot up and looping it round the bitts on the fo'c's'lehead to prevent it sliding back into the sea.

As each section of chain was dropped down the hole, Tessa knew she was nearer salvation, but every time a length of it suddenly shot off the deck she would stop looking.

It was later that she noticed that Joseph was hauling up the chain with more ease. She called up to Ted.

'It's getting easier,' she shouted.

The frown on Ted's face visibly unfolded.

'That means we're above the anchor,' he hollered down to her. 'Only about another eighty feet of chain to go, at a guess.'

'How much is that in metres?'

He paused. 'About twenty-five.'

She forced herself to smile, even though she was dying inside. But when she returned to peer over the coaming she was cheered to see relief on Joseph's face. Instead of having to put his back into it he was pulling in the chain, hand over hand.

'We've got it!' he yelled to them over his shoulder.

'Better get the main up, well reefed.'

Unable to take her eyes off the pile of chain which was heaped up on the deck and growing rapidly higher, Tessa could feel the excitement welling up inside her. When the anchor appeared over the side, a cry of sheer exhilaration erupted from her throat.

Ted leapt on deck.

Tessa climbed up on the back step nearest her and stopped the tiller from swinging. As she grabbed it she heard movement in the cabin. She glanced down quickly. Her uncle was by the galley, shakily pouring water from a big plastic container into a mug and swallowing some pills. Within seconds he had stumbled backwards out of sight and she turned to find Ted helping Joseph back into the cockpit.

Joseph collapsed on the floor, his legs spread-eagled, his back against the lockers. He looked as ashen as her uncle. She stared at him alarmed. 'Is everything all right?'

He nodded. 'Shackled down,' he gasped. 'It shouldn't give us any more trouble.'

Ted returned on deck and began hauling up the mainsail. Gradually the colour began to return to Joseph's face, but his arms and legs continued to shake uncontrollably. He caught sight of her staring at him and gave her a weak smile.

'Just tired,' he explained.

She nodded, attempting to smile back. What on earth was she going to do now? she thought. She couldn't ask him in this state.

'Frightened?' he asked croakily.

'A bit.'

'We'll survive.'

'Joseph,' she began, 'I need . . . would it be all right if . . .'
She reddened.

'Do you want to go to the lavatory?'

She blushed and then to her amazement she added, 'But
there's no hurry.'

Luckily he ignored her.

They made their way along the deck and Joseph went
down into the Heads leaving Tessa on all fours gripping
the edge of the open trapdoor. He gathered up an
armful of the jib and pushed the remaining sail further
against the cabin door to make more space around the
lavatory seat.

The Heads was a small white painted cabin. Its wooden
sides curved in towards a dark mahogany bench and beyond
to a dark recess behind it where ropes and old life-jackets
were stored. A porcelain lavatory bowl was in the centre of
the bench and on one side of it were various levers.

'I'm opening the sea-cocks to let some water in,' Joseph
explained. 'After you've been, pump this lever up and
down. That'll empty it out into the sea. Don't forget to shut
the sea-cocks off after you've finished, or you'll flood the
boat.' He frowned. 'You're looking worried. Would you
rather I did it? It's no trouble.'

'No thanks, I'll do it myself.'

He rummaged around under the staysail, dumped a roll of loo-paper on the top of it and hauled himself up through the hatchway dragging festoons of jib after him.

Tessa lowered herself in, stretching her legs out, but she was too small to reach anything. Joseph gripped her arms and dropped her into the staysail.

'Call whcn you're ready,' he said, peering down at her and he threw her oilskin trousers after her and closed the hatch.

With the wind shut off outside it felt quite snug in the secluded little cabin.

'Privacy,' she whispered.

Ten minutes later, she was still sitting balanced on the sloping wooden seat staring at the brass lock on the small mahogany door in front of her. She had controlled her bladder for so long that her body had gone on strike. She buried her head in her hands, too numbed with cold and tiredness to cry.

The boat suddenly leaned to the other side. They must be changing tack. She braced her legs and looked around the cabin. It was surprisingly restful to be surrounded by creaking wood, with water gurgling beneath her in the bilges, or rushing past the hull outside. She glanced at the outboard motor lashed and bolted underneath the left porthole. The right porthole was under water.

Relieved at being able to drop the artificial smile she had fought to keep fixed since they had left Rye, she felt her face relax. It was at that moment that her body suddenly remembered how to work.

She flushed the lavatory, turned the sea-cocks off, and dragged the oilskin trousers over her jeans, forcing the Guernsey down inside. The trousers came up to her armpits. She slipped the short braces over her shoulders, folded the bottoms up, and quickly put on the oilskin jacket.

Then she sat on the sail, the tweed cap in her hands, and stared out of the left porthole.

Mesmerised by the white foam bursting from green wave after green wave, she caught a glimpse of tiny houses in the distance perched high on vast rocky cliffs. The sky was tinged blood-red by the sun. She watched its fiery glow fall steadily until it disappeared behind the cliffs.

She leaned back into the folds of the staysail. She liked being in this little cabin. It was the only part of the entire nightmarish trip she had liked. Gradually, shadows began to lengthen across the white walls and she knew she would have to return to the cockpit before it grew took dark. With little heart she clambered up and pushed open the hatch. Immediately a blast of cold wind lifted her hair skywards. She shoved the cap on and yelled for Joseph.

A mug of tea and a ham and lettuce sandwich made with two hunks of wholemeal bread was waiting for her in the cockpit. As she tore into it and swallowed the hot liquid, she experienced such a rush of warmth in her stomach that it bordered on bliss.

She glanced up at the mainsail which had been reefed.

'Don't worry, we're well snugged down,' said Joseph, noticing. 'We've avoided having too much sail in case we can't handle it. We're playing safe, even though it'll take us longer.'

'A hell of a sight longer,' added Ted, and he gave Joseph a grin.

Joseph was beaming.

Tessa gasped at them amazed. They actually looked as if they were getting a kick out of it! How could being tossed around in this cockpit in a biting wind, and being soaked by spray when you were least expecting it, how could they possibly find it enjoyable?

Joseph was holding a chart. He folded it to stop it flapping.

'See this, Tessa,' he said, jabbing at it, 'these are the shipping lanes. We've got to avoid them. It can be as busy out here as rush-hour on the M1.'

She stared at him in disbelief.

'Look!' he said, pointing to her left.

She turned and was surprised to find lights dotted all over the place. He picked up a small round black object with a cord attached to it from the shelf under the doghouse. It looked like a miniature car tyre filled with glass. He hung it round his neck, held it horizontally and peered through a small opening at the side.

'What are you doing?' she asked.

'Taking a compass bearing of that,' he said, glancing over her shoulder.

She looked to where he was peering and screamed. Looming towards them in the dusk like a moving mountain was a monstrous oil-tanker.

'We're going to collide!' she shrieked. 'We'll be crushed!'

'No we won't,' said Joseph calmly. 'Here, come and look through this,' and he hung the compass round her neck.

Tessa drew it slowly up to her eyes.

3

Four hours later she was staring bleakly into the inky darkness as the boat slipped behind high black waves. As it rose she could make out a long line of tiny lights in the distance.

Ted was at the helm. Joseph was below. She heard him coming back up the steps.

'Is he all right?' she asked anxiously.

'His pulse feels regular.'

'Did he take the tea?' asked Ted.

Joseph shook his head.

'But he must be so dehydrated,' Ted exclaimed. 'He's brought up everything he's swallowed.'

'He's sleeping like a baby,' said Joseph. 'If he wasn't, then I'd agree with you and send up a flare.'

'What's a flare?' Tessa asked.

'A red rocket. The coastguards look out for them in case people need help.' He turned to Ted. 'I'm sure he'll survive.'

Ted nodded silently. Joseph came and leaned on the coaming next to her.

'Hastings,' he commented, when the lights came back into view.

'And those?' she asked, pointing out to sea.

'Fishing boats.'

As the boat dipped again and the dark waves obliterated them from sight, Tessa raised the hood of her oilskin. Her ears were still aching from the wind. The boat rose again.

'Any of those Mars Bars left?' she heard Ted ask.

'One,' Joseph answered. 'I thought we could split it three ways later when we need some instant energy.'

Three ways, she noted, not four. So they were acting as though she was invisible. She returned to light gazing. She wouldn't ask any more questions. She was obviously still considered a nuisance.

'He's moving!' said Ted suddenly.

They peered down into the dark. Her uncle had stumbled back towards the stove. Probably looking for more pills, Tessa thought. They stared at him motionless, not daring to talk, as though he was a sleepwalker they didn't want to wake suddenly. Transfixed, they watched him fumbling with the drawer under the worktop, but instead of taking out pills he drew out the remaining Mars Bar, ripped the paper off and frantically bit into it. He was halfway through eating it when he lurched backwards, dropped the remainder of the bar on to the floor, and promptly vomited into his bucket.

Within seconds he was back in his bunk. There was a stunned silence.

'I wouldn't have minded if he'd kept it down,' grumbled Ted.

'What a waste,' sighed Joseph, and he glanced at Tessa. 'Sorry.'

It was then that she realised that the *three* had included her! She shrugged valiantly. 'That's OK,' she said.

'Ever seen a cloud with a silver lining?' he asked.

She smiled. 'No.' Was he trying to tell her there was more chocolate somewhere else?

'Look up and you will.'

She glanced up at the sky and gave an involuntary gasp. Underneath the clouds was a silvery glow.

'What makes it look like that?'

'The moon's behind it. It's beautiful, isn't it?'

She nodded. It was.

Suddenly the boat pitched violently, throwing her back into the side of the cockpit. She gripped the coaming and was about to look up at the sky again when she spotted a shadowy head emerge from the sea.

'There's a dead body in the water!' she shrieked.

'Where?' yelled Ted from above.

She pointed wildly at it. He gave a short laugh.

'It's a dolphin!'

She squinted and looked again. He was right.

The two men leaned excitedly over the coaming.

'Extraordinary!' cried Joseph.

The dark shape bobbed up and down a few times by the port bow and then disappeared.

'I wonder if it'll stay with us,' said Ted.

'I've never seen a dolphin outside a zoo before!' Tessa exclaimed.

'Me neither,' added Joseph.

They peered out into the night, trying to catch sight of it again.

Tessa gave a yawn.

'Joseph,' said Ted suddenly, 'we ought to have watches.'

'We can't take naps with Nick ill,' Joseph began, 'although . . .' And he glanced at Tessa. 'Think you could take the helm while one of us deals with the sail on a tack? Being a cutter she needs two people to handle her.'

Flattered, Tessa nodded.

'She'll need sleep too,' said Ted.

'Of course. We can take it in turns.'

Joseph let her use his sleeping-bag on the top bunk, opposite the bunk where her uncle slept. There was so little space that she had to wriggle into it on her back. She took off Joseph's Guernsey and made herself a pillow with it. It was strange lying down next to a porthole and seeing nothing but sea beside her.

She was convinced she wouldn't be able to fall asleep

– conditions at sea made everything feel too damp – but as soon as she began to feel warm she was dragged instantly into unconsciousness.

Occasionally she awoke to feel the cool breeze from the open hatch on the cabin roof drifting across her face. She tried to roll over on to her side but she ached too much to move. Once when she woke, she discovered that a blanket had been tucked round her and there was a soft light in the cabin. She raised her head to see where it was coming from. Joseph was leaning over the chart table, an old woolly hat on, writing in a logbook. The light was coming from a small oil-lamp swinging from the hook by his head.

It was much later when she woke properly. She peered out of the porthole only to find the dark waves still crashing against the glass.

She wriggled out of the sleeping-bag and lowered herself over the side into her canvas shoes. Shivering, she drew the warm Guernsey back over her head. She glanced over at her uncle and observed the rise and fall of his chest. He was still alive. Grabbing the cap and oilskins she staggered towards the cockpit, reaching out with her free hand for anything solid she could take hold of to support her.

As soon as she stepped out of the cabin, the cold wind socked her with such force it sent her reeling. Joseph was at the helm, standing on the deck. Ted was taking a bearing.

'What time is it?' she asked.

'Half past threeish,' said Ted.

'I'm ready to help if one of you wants a sleep.'

'Not me,' said Ted.

'I wouldn't mind a kip,' said Joseph.

Ted took over at the helm and Joseph went below. Tessa hurriedly dragged on her oilskins and stuck her cap on. Ted asked her to look out for a particular light. She stared intently into the darkness, her fingers frozen as she gripped the coaming.

Though noisy and awe-inspiring, the waves had a peaceful quality to them. Each time they slapped the boat, an icy spray would smack her in the face, but it was pointless to protest and soon she found herself accepting having soaked oilskins, a damp cap and water dripping from her numbed nose. For the first time in months, gazing out at the unending sea, her homework faded into insignificance.

She was surprised to see Joseph step out of the cabin.

'Couldn't you sleep?' she asked.

'I only needed a quick snooze. I feel much better now. Fancy some tea?'

Tessa beamed. 'Yes, please!'

It was later, while warming her hands round her mug, that she was suddenly dazzled by a brilliant white light sweeping across the sea. Behind the dim glow which followed it, she could see soaring chalky-white cliffs. It was a spectacular sight. Within seconds, the light swept across the waves again and the cliffs came back into view.

'Beachy Head,' said Joseph.

'Isn't that near Newhaven?'

'Yes and no. It's about eight miles.'

'But eight miles is close.'

'In a car it is, not out at sea, and not when you're having to tack as slowly as we are.'

'Why don't we motor-sail?' suggested Ted.

'That's not a bad idea. I'll check the engine hasn't any water in it.'

The engine was fine. As soon as Tessa heard it chug into life, it was all she could do not to sing. She would never have believed that the sound of an old engine could have given her so much pleasure.

The feeling did not last. The engine gave a clunk and then there was silence.

Tessa pressed herself against the back of the cockpit and slid down on to one of the steps. Joseph fiddled with the gearbox and then began lifting up floorboards and prodding and banging in the bilges. Tessa tried to see what he was doing, but it was too dark.

She listened, her fingers crossed tightly, but aside from the occasional cough, the engine remained ominously quiet.

'I think there must be something caught up in the screw,' he remarked at last.

He dived into the cabin and returned with a boat-hook. Leaning over the coaming he thrust it over the side. Within seconds he gave a loud yell. The boat-hook was being dragged out of his hand. Ted leapt towards him and grabbed it. Tessa instantly jumped up and steadied the tiller. She was surprised at how confident and at home she felt. At school and at home she was always being told how slowly she responded. Now she seemed to move before she thought.

'Thanks,' said Ted when he took it from her.

She noticed they were none too happy.

'We've found out what it is. A huge piece of industrial plastic,' Joseph explained. 'There's no way we can sort it out until we're moored.'

'You mean we can't use the engine?' Tessa exclaimed.

'No. So it's sailing all the way. At least the tide will be washing us in once we reach Newhaven.'

'I don't think we'd better mention this to Nick,' said Ted quietly.

They reached Newhaven at midday. It had been sunny all morning, but out at sea the warmth failed to penetrate Tessa's frozen limbs. It wasn't till they entered the channel that Tessa grew so hot that she had to take off her oilskins.

Sailing slowly down it, dwarfed on either side by the seventy-feet-high pierheads, Tessa shaded her eyes and looked upwards for signs of life, but it was useless. The colossal walls of steel and timber were twice the height of the mast and only if she was lucky did she catch sight of someone's head.

As they dawdled along, all sails up, whilst countless vessels motored speedily past them, Tessa gazed mesmerised at the mass of glistening seaweed hanging like slapping ribbons from the black, rust-stained bulks. Beneath the seaweed, thousands of sharp barnacles were stuck like a collage of giant shells against it.

The mainsail hardly moved. They were so sheltered they were lucky to get breeze-power let alone wind-power. Twice they lost steerage completely. It was as if they had no rudder. No matter what Ted and Joseph tried to do, the boat swung completely out of their control and began to point out to sea. People from passing vessels screamed out at them from their cockpits as Joseph and Ted repeatedly yelled back, 'We've no engine!'

While Joseph helmed, she and Ted would stand on deck with boat-hooks ready to fend off if they were thrown too close to a pierhead or other boats. Then a gust would catch the sails and they would be in control again.

As soon as they reached the marina, the mainsail was dropped and Joseph leapt with a rope across a massive gap on to the jetty. The only way the boat could be manoeuvred into a berth was for him to walk round the moored boats and pull theirs into a space between two others. Tessa could not bear to look. Having come this far she couldn't take any more disasters. She turned her back and hastily busied herself tying the mainsail to the boom.

Even after they had found a berth and she had glimpsed Joseph out of the corner of her eye readjusting the ropes which tied them to the catwalk, Tessa still could not bring herself to watch. It wasn't till after he and Ted had helped with the remainder of the mainsail that she turned and stared at the catwalk in disbelief. After being at sea for over twenty-four hours she still couldn't believe they had made it. She surveyed the marina. Hundreds of metal masts glinted in the sunlight and the air was filled with a cacophony of jingling sounds like lots of little chinese bells ringing. She had never heard anything so lovely.

Joseph didn't seem to be taking much notice of them. He was too busy tying the old tyres back over the side.

'What's that noise?' she asked.

'The halyards.'

'What are they?'

'The ropes we pull the sails up with. If they're not tied down, the breeze catches them and they jangle. Haven't you ever heard them before?'

'No. The only boats I've been around are at indoor boat shows. There's no breeze there.'

'Like it?'

She smiled. 'Yes.'

As she gazed at all the gleaming polished boats she was surprised to discover that she didn't envy them. In fact they didn't seem like real boats at all, more like floating caravans. She noticed a few people appearing in their cockpits and staring in their direction and she found herself feeling a mixture of amusement and pride. The cutter was the only boat in sight which had a wooden mast. It might be an ancient tub, she thought, but it had looked after them in wild seas and fierce winds and brought them home.

'Tessa!'

She turned.

'Ted and I are going to a café we know to have breakfast. Coming?'

'I haven't any money.'

'On us.'

'Yes, please. I'm starving. But what about my uncle?'

'He's still breathing steadily. We'll leave a note and tell him where we are in case he wakes.'

As she clambered off the boat and on to the catwalk she felt the wooden boards move rapidly under her feet. She leaned quickly to one side to regain her balance.

'I didn't realise this was a floating catwalk,' she said, surprised. 'I thought it was fixed.'

Ted grinned. 'It is.'

'But it's moving. I can feel it tipping me over.'

'No it isn't,' Joseph laughed. 'You've found your sea legs, that's all. If you think this is moving, wait till you sit at a table and try to eat.'

Joseph was right. Sitting in the café, trying to tuck into a cooked breakfast was like trying to play chess on deck in a gale-force wind. Every time she glanced down at her eggs and bacon, the table rose up and then tipped to one side. Once they had finished eating she couldn't wait to get back on to the boat.

Her uncle was still sleeping deeply when they staggered back into the cabin. Speechless with tiredness, they gave him a cursory glance before crawling swiftly into their sleeping-bags, except for Joseph who wrapped a blanket round himself in the bunk underneath Tessa. Ted lay on the top bunk opposite.

It was some time later that she was woken out of a deep sleep by voices on the catwalk. Somebody was recounting one of his sailing adventures. She listened for a moment before closing her eyes.

'We were pitching so violently,' she heard him say, 'it wrenched out the wooden shoe. Next thing we knew the anchor had gone overboard and the chain was rushing after it.'

Poor bloke, thought Tessa drowsily, knowing what he must have been through.

'Oh no!' said another male voice. 'What the hell did you do?'

Tessa had hardly fallen back to sleep again when the voices pulled her back into consciousness.

'Too risky returning to Rye,' the man continued, 'so we kept sailing through the night against tremendous winds.'

Tessa rolled over sleepily and peered through the porthole. A pair of yellow boots was pacing up and down the catwalk. She guessed they belonged to the story-teller.

'That must have been frightening,' commented another member of his audience.

The man laughed. 'It was. Let's face it, anyone who says they're not frightened in those circumstances must be lying.'

Tessa yawned and attempted to get back to sleep, but as the man on the catwalk continued to give a graphic account of his trip from Rye to Newhaven, Tessa began to find the story vaguely familiar. She leaned over the edge of her bunk and looked down.

Her uncle's bunk was empty.

'I don't believe it!' she muttered, amazed.

Looking up she discovered that Ted was also awake. He was beaming. From underneath her bunk there was an explosion of laughter.

'How can you?' she protested. 'He didn't lift a finger and there he is out there acting as if he sailed this boat single-handed. Aren't you going to stop him?'

Joseph poked his head out, a broad smile on his face.

'He has to have some pleasures from sailing,' he said.

'But he's telling lies!' And then she stopped. 'Wait a minute. Has he done this before?'

'Sort of,' said Joseph. 'It's just that he likes the idea of sailing and all the things associated with it, but if the water isn't as still as a mill-pond, he's seasick.'

'Seasick! You mean that illness was just seasickness?'

'Seasickness can be very debilitating.'

'Seasick!' she spluttered.

'Nelson used to get seasick,' said Ted.

'You're joking! Really?'

Joseph nodded.

'Well he's not going to get away with it this time. The stories he's told my family. Ooh I'm so cross!' And she threw herself on to her back and scowled.

'And just as we were approaching Newhaven,' she heard her uncle say, 'the engine stopped.'

'Oh. Bad luck,' chorused his listeners.

'Seawater got inside?' asked one.

'No. Some industrial plastic caught up in the screw. Nearly took the boat-hook. And us.'

This was greeted with laughter.

'You wait,' muttered Tessa through gritted teeth. She closed her eyes and willed his voice into oblivion. 'You'll get your come-uppance later.'

As she lay there, rehearsing all the insults she was going to hurl at him, she was suddenly aware again of the jangling halyards in the marina. She touched the beams above her head and then turned to look at the tiny bookcase behind her. It was filled with old paperbacks. She gazed at the chronometer with its bronze surround on the wall beside the door to the Heads, and at the hatch and at all the old creaking wood which surrounded her, and she knew she would never betray her uncle to her parents. If she did, they would be so horrified they would never let her go sailing with him again. In that moment she realised she was hooked, that her life would never be the same again. The sea hadn't just entered her legs, it had seeped into her bloodstream. She glanced at Ted. He was asleep.

'Joseph,' she said quietly.

'Mm?'

'I've decided not to say anything after all.'

'I thought you'd change your mind. Think you'd like to come again?'

'Can I?'

He laughed. 'Of course.'

She took a last look through the porthole. Her uncle's boots were still marching up and down the catwalk and he was still expounding.

'But I'll never ever wear yellow wellies,' she said with determination. 'I'll save up for blue ones instead.' And with that she closed her eyes and allowed the cutter to rock her creakily back to sleep.

Head Race

'You stupid berk, they're going to get past us!'

'I told you we should have had a girl cox,' said the Number Four, exasperated. 'They think more quickly.'

'I don't believe this,' moaned the Number Two, looking over his shoulder as another eight whisked easily past them.

'We should be in that current!' yelled the Number Three oarsman.

Ben stared miserably at the eight exhausted men in front of him.

Other boats skimmed by. The wash tossed their boat chaotically, sending water slopping over the sides.

Ben's trainers were soaked and the life-jacket he was wearing for padding had risen up high on to his shoulders making him feel like an American footballer and exposing the very part of his body which needed most protection.

As the boat jerked forward at each pull of the crew's blades, the piece of wood which jutted out behind him seemed to gouge out lumps of skin from the small of his back.

And now they had all started shouting at him again.

When they had done it earlier, Ben had put it down to

nerves from having had to wait so long at the beginning of the race. Because there were over three hundred boats entering the Head, it had to be staggered. They were number 183. Sitting huddled together, hemmed in by the other boats, they had grown stiffer and tenser by the minute.

They'd had a jerky start but no jerkier than anyone else so that Ben had been totally unprepared for the sudden onslaught of venom from his crew. Screaming, 'Over to the right, you blithering idiot!' at him and, 'No, you cretin, to the left!' Ben had gaped at them, stunned, as they had shot towards him on their seats, hollering.

Even when they slid away from him pulling their blades through the water there was no relief. They still glared at him and within seconds they were all shooting forward in his direction again and he would find himself almost nose to nose with Stroke.

And then there was the pain.

With each accelerated jerk the small of his back was repeatedly hit. It was all he could do not to cry out. Instead he blushed furiously as the eight yelling men continued to propel themselves towards him and away again.

Was this the pleasant-tempered team he had trained with on those balmy evenings on the river? he had asked himself. But then on their training sessions they hadn't taken much notice of him. They had been too busy listening to their coach as he rode along the bank on his bicycle issuing instructions through a loudspeaker. And there had been few boats to bother them. They had had mostly only herons for company. Eventually, to his relief, they had settled into a steady rhythm, leaving Ben to steer them among the flotilla of boats streaming jaggedly down the river.

He tried to relax, but his forehead ached from frowning away the sun which was bouncing off the water into his eyes. He pulled down the peak of cap but it only meant he had to raise his chin to keep an eye on the crew.

He tried to change position in the tiny space, drawing his knees even closer to his chest. Huddled into a tight ball his legs felt so stiff he wondered if he'd ever walk again.

He gazed forward at the long slim boat which now seemed about a mile long. The broad-shouldered Number Four was baring his teeth at him. He was the tallest of the men and mega-serious. He came in for weight and circuit training at least three or four times a week.

Stroke trained seriously too, but usually he enjoyed it. Now he too was staring at Ben grim-faced.

It was all right for them, thought Ben. He had to learn on his own. They could easily find people to coach them so they could improve their rowing. Finding someone to coach a cox was impossible.

He felt pent up with frustration. He wanted to help them but he wasn't sure what to tell them. He didn't even have his dad to help patch up his mistakes.

He mustn't panic, he told himself fiercely. He must keep reminding himself that he was in charge, but it felt strange at only thirteen to be telling a crew of thirty to forty-year-olds what to do. Some of them were even older than his father.

'Now what are you doing?' yelled the Number Four again. 'Move us over!'

Ben knew they couldn't move yet. They would have had to cut a corner. Dad said he must never do that. Besides, he had a vague feeling they would be heading for dead water.

'Give us the orders, come on!' joined the Number Seven. 'Use your bloody eyes!!'

And then they all joined in, including Stroke.

Ben lost his nerve. He glanced quickly behind him. Perhaps they were right. After all, they were more experienced.

He started to give out orders to the individual oarsmen.

They slowed down. They were in dead water. His instinct had been right.

'Couldn't you see there's no current here?' yelled the Number Two.

'But you asked me . . .' he began.

'You're not supposed to obey us,' snapped Stroke. 'We're supposed to obey you. Now get us out of here.'

Two eights swept past them, their blades narrowly missing clashing against theirs.

'In. Out,' yelled Ben, his voice shaking with anger and hurt. 'In. Out.'

'Now where are you taking us?' screamed the Number Four.

'Only to the middle of the river,' panted the Number Seven. 'Take us to the fastest part.'

The middle is the fastest part, thought Ben. At least, that's what he thought. But then nobody seemed to know for sure. Everyone had their theories, which all conflicted with one another.

'Watch out,' yelled a cox from a nearby boat. Ben gave the individual orders to straighten out.

'Right,' he muttered. 'Since everything I do is a mistake, I might as well make a big one. In. Out,' he yelled quickly. 'Come on! Keep together!'

'You're taking us too fast,' gasped Stroke.

'In. Out,' repeated Ben, ignoring him.

They were really moving now. Ben was right. The middle of the river was faster, and with the additional rowing speed they were moving at a tremendous pace.

'We'll never keep this up,' said the Number Two.

'Quiet in the boat,' yelled Ben. 'You're wasting energy.'

And then they hit a mooring buoy.

Ben didn't care. In the distance, he could see the bend in the river. There were two eights behind him and one ahead. He had to get in between them otherwise they would be left behind and thrown back into dead water. He knew he had to time it so that their boat was near the edge when they went round the bend. He could see from what the other eights were doing that they all agreed that that was where the fastest bit of the river was.

He gave the orders to move.

They were moving too fast to avoid another buoy. It clunked against the side of the boat and rocked wildly.

He could hear furious yells coming from somewhere and he knew they were aimed at him.

'That's their water,' said Stroke alarmed, referring to the boat behind them. 'If we move into that we'll be disqualified.'

Now he tells me, thought Ben.

Within seconds he steered to the starboard side.

'Oh my giddy aunt!' panted the quieter Number Three. 'Make up your mind will you?'

A crew of eight passed them. Out of the corner of his eye Ben saw them swerve too close to the bank. They careered into one of the moored houseboats knocking one of the blades out. As the blade went flying in the air, Ben could see the crew angrily waving their fists at their girl cox even though it wasn't her fault.

Ben felt for her. Being a cox was like being a human punch-bag.

'Watch out!' yelled an eight on their port side.

They didn't make it to the edge of the water.

His crew were furious. Ben could understand why. Working as hard as they could they had to endure seeing other crews not making so much effort but moving faster because they had been coxed into the fast current.

'In. Out,' yelled Ben, his voice growing hoarse.

'Now where are we going?' yelled out the Number Two.

Luckily, being a veteran team, their boat didn't rate having a cox box-loudspeaker. Otherwise his muttered, 'I haven't the faintest idea,' would have resounded all down the river.

By some fluke, they found themselves back in good water and were picking up speed.

'In. Out,' he yelled. 'In. Out.'

They were racing along at a fantastic rate. It was wonderful. His spirits soared. At last he had done it. It had taken him nearly the whole race to get it together, but they hadn't been disqualified or capsized or lost a blade.

He grinned with the sheer exhilaration of it.

Until he saw the eight ahead.

It didn't take him long to work out that their crew were not rowing as fast as his. In fact, they looked spent. What was he to do? His crew were rowing magnificently, their blades rising out of the water in perfect unison, turning and scooping the water in beautiful measured time.

If he made them slow down all their hard work would go for nothing. If he didn't, they would crash straight into the boat in front. He continued to urge them on. He knew he was being stupid, but he couldn't stop himself. He was hoping for a flash of inspiration or that somehow they would be able to fly.

Someone in the crew in front started to point wildly over their cox's shoulder. The cox glanced swiftly round with a look of horror.

Within seconds, she was giving orders for her crew to move out of the way.

Ben watched his boat heading directly towards its stern. They were almost on top of them. As they passed them, their oars clashed.

'Keep calm,' yelled Ben. 'In. Out. In. Out!'

And then they were through and he heard the crew they had scorched past fall yelling into the water and he knew they had capsized.

He glanced at his team. To his amazement, his Number Four and Number Seven were smiling. They were the only members of his team who were. The others looked as if they were wondering whether to put up their life insurance subscriptions or take up golf instead.

To his shame, Ben still didn't care. He concentrated on getting his crew back into a steady rhythm. They had beaten another eight. It seemed daft to get so excited about it when there were so many boats in the Head Race. But he had coxed them into good water and kept them there.

The crew were beginning to flag, their vests sodden with sweat. The Number Five looked so red that if the top of his head had popped off, Ben wouldn't have been surprised to have seen steam erupting from it.

Ahead of them was a bridge. Beyond that it was a mere hundred metres to the club's pontoon.

'Keep together,' Ben yelled. 'Drive with your legs!'

He had heard one of the older coxes use that expression so he thought he'd chuck it in for good measure.

'We're nearly home,' he yelled.

'I'm not going to make it,' groaned the Number Five.

'Of course you're going to make it,' Ben screamed. 'You're rowing fantastically. Come on. Keep going. In. Out. In. Out.'

And they were back into a steady rhythm again, everyone pulling in unison.

It was at that moment that another eight appeared. They were a schoolboy team. At a glance Ben figured that the oldest couldn't be older than fifteen or sixteen. To Ben's amazement he saw 302 emblazoned on the back of the cox. They must have started way after them and here they were gracefully gliding alongside them.

His Number Four and Number Seven jutted their jaws out in anger.

'Come on,' yelled Number Four. 'They're beating us! Get us in the right water.'

But Ben knew it wasn't because they weren't in good water. The schoolboy team was faster because they were better, fitter, and younger.

'Come on, keep going,' he yelled hoarsely. 'We can do it!'

'We're going as hard as we can,' panted out the Number Five angrily.

'In. Out. In. Out,' screamed Ben. 'Push your paddles away!'

But it was no use. The schoolboy team was past them and everyone in his crew was calling Ben every four letter word Ben knew, and a few he didn't.

Ben was so panic-stricken that he didn't see through his eight burly crew a boat stopping in front of them. By sheer fluke they missed it, but only just.

'Are you going to bloody cox us or not?' yelled Number Four.

'Give me strength!' roared Number Seven.

'Look behind you,' yelled Stroke.

Ben took a quick look. Several eights were skimming towards them. In the time it took him to whirl round, Ben realised that they were boxed in at the side by even faster eights, sending them swaying to the starboard side of the river directly towards the bridge.

He couldn't order his crew to slow down. They'd be hit from behind. Visions of other people's flailing blades concussing his exhausted crew descended on him.

With horror he watched his crew speed towards the bridge.

'We're going to hit the bridge!' he yelled.

'Stop us then, you berk.'

How can I? thought Ben. We're hemmed in.

It was weird. He knew they were hurtling along, yet it seemed as if they had suddenly gone into slow motion.

He swallowed.

'Go easy,' he said weakly.

Should he get them to drop their blades into the water to slow them down? No, they'd still crash and some of the blades were bound to get broken. As he tried to think of a way out, he suddenly realised that they were making no headway. He had lost steerage. The rudder was simply refusing to obey him. Helpless he watched the boat swing round like a piece of driftwood.

'Drop your blades!' he screeched.

The current was bringing them down nearer the bridge, broadside on.

'Fend off!'

They hit the bridge. The boat gave a huge jolt. The short stocky Number Six lost grip on his blade. The handle swung back wildly, hitting him hard under the chin and sending him sprawling backwards with such force that his head hit the Number Five squarely in the belly.

Already a deep red, the Number Five's face turned instantly purple. Ben stared horrified at him as he opened and shut his mouth, fighting for breath. It looked as though he was going to have a heart attack on his hands and he wouldn't even be able to get to him to give him the kiss of life.

The boat gave a sudden lurch. Stroke, now ashen, leaned towards Ben and vomited.

Ben clung to the sides of the boat as it rocked, the peak of his cap and his clothes dripping. And he came to a decision. He would not look down.

In an instant he realised that they still had a chance. The boat hadn't sunk and none of the blades had been broken. But most important of all, they were still moving. If they had stopped it would have taken his crew for ever to get their shocked muscles into gear again.

The pontoon was only a hundred metres away. A hundred metres and it would all be over.

He grappled for something to say. He had heard one of the more experienced coxes in their club yell, 'Take me home,' when her crew had almost reached the end of a race.

What he hadn't realised was that it was the sort of command you gave in a regatta to a crew who were lengths ahead of the only other crew. The command gave them a chance to relax and catch their breaths before their final winning spurt.

As Ben watched his crew floundering and attempting to push themselves away, he yelled with as much of a commanding voice as he could muster.

'Take me home!'

'Shut up, you little punk,' yelled the Number Two.

'Did he say "Take me home"?' screamed the Number Four. 'I'll take him home all right. I'll take him to the bloody cleaners.'

'We haven't got eyes in the backs of our heads,' said the Number Three. 'Give us some instructions!'

Ben gulped.

With so many boats streaming past them, they sat, their

blades held clear of the water while the wash sent them rocking violently back to the wall of the bridge.

'If you don't get us moving,' rasped Stroke in his face, 'we'll stop altogether and we'll never get started again.'

Ben spotted the tiniest gap appearing between two boats.

'Paddle on One and Three. Pull,' he yelled, and he cased the rudder gently.

But his crew were falling apart. The sudden episode with the bridge after the frenzy of rowing had left them uncoordinated.

Ben crossed his fingers. 'Come on everyone. In. Out. In. Out.'

By a miracle they somehow managed to pull themselves into the gap. Sluggishly and laboriously they headed for the pontoon.

'Never again,' muttered Ben, sponging down the hull of the boat with wide angry strokes. 'Never, never again!'

Ever since he had started washing the boat down he had been trying to wipe out the memory of their arrival at the pontoon.

Having swallowed down his embarrassment, he had had to go through the whole procedure of telling them to unscrew the blades and pick the boat up out of the water. While they had carried it coffin-like on their shoulders to the section of the field apportioned to their club's boats, the umpire had stopped them to tell him off for hitting two buoys and to disqualify them for causing a boat to capsize.

But it hadn't been that which had incensed his crew. Or the crash into the bridge. It was the fact that they had been beaten by a crew of schoolboys which had left them smarting.

Once the boat had been stacked they had surrounded Ben and towered over him haranguing him.

Even mild-mannered Stroke was fuming, though he did tell the Number Four to 'lighten up' when he had threatened to spit-roast Ben.

There wasn't even a chance for Ben to apologise, and anyway it seemed pointless. They wouldn't have been in the mood to accept it even if they had heard it.

As soon as they had abandoned him to take their showers, Ben began his usual task of cleaning down the boat. It was part of a cox's duties. A crew was always too exhausted to do it.

He threw the sponge into the bucket and rested his head on the boat for a moment, still trying to erase all the names he had been called.

A sudden hissing sound made him whirl round with fright.

Peering round a row of boats stacked in tiers behind him, he saw a mop of tangled red hair. It was Mandy, one of the other coxes. She was a year older than him.

'You made me jump. What are you doing?' he asked.

'Hiding.'

'From your crew?'

'No. From Bill. He'll kill me when he finds out what I've done. There's a twelve-foot gash in our boat.'

'What happened?'

'We hit an island. What am I going to do?'

'I don't know. I know what I'll be doing though. I'll be back to rowing with my family. That's if they don't chuck me out of the Rowing Club.'

'Yes. I heard your lot. They were pretty foul, weren't they?'

Ben nodded. 'Dad warned me some of them might throw a wobbly, but I didn't really believe him. No wonder they find it difficult to get a cox. It's a mug's game. Look at this,' he said, presenting the front of his T-shirt. He turned round and hauled it up.

'And this!'

A huge dark bruise fanned out round the base of his spine.

'And I ache everywhere. And for what? A bellyful of flack.'

'At least you're alive,' she said encouragingly. 'And no one got drowned, did they?'

'No,' he said miserably. 'But my chances of coxing in a race again have been scuppered.'

'You mean you want to go through it again?' asked Mandy, amazed.

'Yes,' he said, surprised. 'I suppose I do.'

'You're as mad as I am.'

Suddenly, she looked over his shoulder and gave a yelp. Ben swung round. A Land Rover was approaching. The driver was in his forties, tanned and with a thick moustache. It was Bill. He leaned out of the window, smiling with amusement at Mandy, who had taken off at a sprint.

'What's up with her?' he called out.

'She thinks you're going to kill her. Her boat's got a huge gash in it.'

To Ben's alarm, Bill leapt out of the car and ran after her.

'Why didn't I keep my big mouth shut?' he muttered.

But in the distance he could hear Bill yelling, 'Hey! Mandy! I can patch that up. No problem. Come back!'

Ben glanced down at his clothes. He smelt terrible. There was no getting away from it. He would have to take a shower. With any luck his crew would have taken theirs by now.

But he picked up the chamois-leather and began rubbing the hull vigorously as another delaying tactic.

There must have been a long queue for the shower, for the first thing Ben heard as he entered the adjoining cloakroom was his crew's voices echoing under the running water.

He sank quickly on to a bench in the corner, hiding himself behind the track suits which had been flung over the hooks.

Gingerly he took off his sodden cap and dropped it on the floor.

He had showered masses of times with other men, so it wasn't out of embarrassment that he was avoiding taking off his clothes. He just wasn't used to showering with his own crew. Usually, after a training session, by the time he had hosed and rubbed down the boat, they were already in the bar having a welcome pint.

Suddenly, the thought of being naked with eight furious men made him feel extremely vulnerable.

A loud roar of laughter from the shower caused him to raise his head. Up till that moment he had managed to shut out the noise.

'And when your head went thwack into my gut,' he heard the Number Five say, 'I thought I'd be pushing up the daisies.'

'So did I,' said the Number Six, wryly.

'What about when he said "Take me home",' put in the Number Five. 'I'll never forget that.'

'Priceless,' added the posh Number Three, and they all fell about laughing again.

Ben was burning with embarrassment.

'I'll live off that for months,' said the Number Seven.

'And did you see the expression on that cox's face when we scraped past her? I couldn't stop smiling.'

Ben was stunned. They were already telling anecdotes about the race as if they had enjoyed it!

'Best Head Race I've been in for years,' said the Bow.

'Yes,' said Stroke. 'Let's hope no one tries to nab him. Any cox is difficult to get, but a good one . . .'

The others voiced their agreement.

Ben couldn't believe it. Was this the man who had snarled at him, called him the cretinous runt of an orangutan, and vomited all over him?

It didn't take Ben long to twig that although their anger had been directed at him, they had really been angry with themselves.

They started to talk about the team who had hit the houseboat and then the Number Four and Number Seven started singing.

Ben could have sung out loud with them. They actually wanted him to cox for them again! Tears of relief blurred his vision. Hastily, he pressed his fingers hard into his eyes in case anyone walked in and saw him.

Once he had pulled himself together, he peeled off his clothes, flung his towel round his waist sarong style, took a deep breath and sauntered casually towards the showers.

Dan

His dad had arranged to meet them near the ticket office at the Leisure Centre, but it was all too obvious when he and his mother had stared at the electronic doors for a quarter of an hour that his dad had been delayed.

'Nothing changes, does it?' his mother remarked at last.

'I expect he's been held up in the traffic,' Daniel protested. 'Saturday's always a bad day on the roads.'

'Every day's a bad day where your dad's concerned.'

'Please, Mum . . .' he began.

'I'll give him a call.'

'Don't start on him. He won't come if you do.'

'Don't worry,' she said, gritting her teeth. 'I'll be as nice as pie.'

Daniel sat on the steps next to the weighing machine and watched her at the payphone. A couple of years ago he wouldn't have believed that a slim-line version of her would be standing in a Leisure Centre, looking quite at home in a blue tracksuit and trainers. She had once been so overweight she had worn nothing but voluminous tent-like dresses. And because she had always been so miserable then, Daniel used to call her the Moaning Marquee. That was before she and his dad separated and divorced. Now he resented her looking so fit.

'Hello, Mike! It's Julie.'

Daniel raised his eyes. His dad didn't need to be told her name.

'Daniel's waiting for you at the Leisure Centre with his swimming gear,' she said with artificial brightness. There was a pause. 'You can always wear dark underpants. No one'll tell the difference.' She was now smiling so hard it looked like a grimace. 'He's been doing a lot of practice. I think he's hoping to get into a swimming team at Royston . . .' The smile faded. 'I didn't choose Royston. He did.' Another pause. 'No, I don't think it was because Royston doesn't have . . .' His mother had now gone red. 'Mike, not many Comprehensives *do* rugby!'

Daniel sank his head into his hands. 'Mum, please,' he begged.

Back came the artificial smile.

'Anyway,' she added gaily, 'I still think you'll be impressed. He has a really good style now . . . OK, I'll tell him . . . Yes, well you'd better answer it then. Bye.'

She came over and leaned on the handrail.

'He says he'll be here in five minutes, but if there really was someone at the door I'd make that ten.'

Daniel nodded. He knew he should be pleased, but instead he felt as though a cement mixer was sitting on his chest.

'You know him, love,' she added softly.

Daniel looked hurriedly away. His eyes had begun to sting and he didn't want her to see.

'You go on home, Mum,' he said. 'I'll be all right.'

'I don't like to leave you here on your own.'

'I won't be alone for very long, will I?'

There was a pause.

'No,' she said quietly.

Because Daniel worshipped his father, his mother had agreed to let him stay with him every weekend, even though some judge had said every three weeks. His dad had his own flat now, so there was a room for Daniel to sleep in.

'I can easily wait,' she said.

'I don't want you to wait!' he snapped.

'OK. OK.'

She put down the rolled-up sleeping bag she was carrying by his feet.

'Take it away. You're embarrassing me.'

'You want somewhere to sleep tonight, don't you?'

'Look, I know he probably won't have had time to make my bed,' Daniel said wearily. 'I told you I don't mind making it myself.'

'That's if you can find it. You know what a slob . . .'

'He is not!' exploded Daniel. 'Just because he's not as tidy as you are . . .'

There was a moment's silence.

'I'll see you tomorrow night then,' she said, kissing the top of his head.

'Yeah,' he grunted.

'If you change your mind about having a go at rowing in the morning, give me a buzz and I'll give you a lift to the boathouse.'

'I won't change my mind.'

She hesitated for a moment, picked up the sleeping bag, and then turned quickly on her heel.

Daniel watched the electronic doors slide open for her. He kept his eyes on her as she walked through the car park, hoping she wouldn't look back. He had made up his mind that, if his father hadn't turned up in ten minutes, he would go to the pool on his own.

He swam thirty lengths. He kidded himself that his dad would have been impressed, even though he knew that only one sport existed for his father.

Before going into the pool, he had undressed with painstaking slowness, expecting him to burst through the door at any moment. Later, when he was swimming, he kept checking to see if he was coming out of the changing rooms. Even as he dried and dressed himself, he half expected to have to put on his wet trunks again and go back in the pool with him. But of course he never came. Daniel stood in the foyer watching people entering and leaving in groups and pairs, chatting and laughing, and he felt a loneliness so overwhelming it physically hurt.

He stared at the payphone, but he couldn't bring himself to dial his father's number in case he answered.

Then he had an idea.

He ran swiftly over to the ticket office. A young woman with long glossy hair smiled down at him.

'Had a good swim?' she asked cheerily.

'Yeah.' And he smiled back. Her happiness was infectious. 'How did you guess?'

'Your hair's wet. Do you want to use one of the courts or the athletics track now?'

'No. I was just wondering if you'd seen a big man come in here in the last half-hour.'

'With a beer belly?'

'Yeah. That's him.'

'He went up to the canteen.' She gave him the directions.

He raced up the stairs, half-stumbling with excitement, weaving in and out of a group of men and women with squash rackets who were coming down.

He burst through the swing doors on the landing and across a long stretch of floor, down a corridor and past the bar. The canteen doors were about ten metres away. He slowed down, his heart beating, slung his bag over his shoulder and strolled towards the door, grinning.

The young woman was right. There was a big man sitting in the canteen, but it wasn't his dad.

Daniel gazed at him in disbelief. The man looked up. Daniel

quickly made for the counter. He would have to buy himself something now. It would look daft if he walked in and out.

'Excuse me!'

A loud voice made him swing round. A tall lean man, dressed in a white singlet, long slim-fitting white trousers which hooked over the feet and white canvas shoes which looked like a cross between plimsolls and ballet shoes, was standing at the door.

'I only have three people in my trampoline group,' he announced. 'Seems everyone is away on holiday. I need a fourth person to cover one side otherwise I'll have to cancel and send the others home. Any chance of a volunteer?'

'Not me, mate,' boomed the tank he'd wished was his dad.

The man laughed. 'That's all right, I was hoping for someone younger.'

Daniel wasn't quite sure what it was that made him raise his arm. Maybe it was the silence which made him feel awkward. But he hardly had any time to regret it because the beam on the man's face made him feel he had handed him the Crown Jewels.

'Great!' he said.

Daniel ambled shyly towards him.

'I really appreciate you giving us your time,' said the man as they squeezed through the doorway together.

It was while they were striding down the long open space towards the swing doors that the man put his hand on Daniel's shoulder. Normally Daniel would have been acutely embarrassed, but there was something in the man's manner which made him feel relaxed. 'My name's Stewart,' he said. 'What's yours?'

Daniel was about to say 'Titch'. It was what everyone called him, including the teachers, at his junior school. Did. He wouldn't be seeing them again. He would be starting at the Royston Road comprehensive in a month.

'Dan,' he said suddenly. It was like putting on a new identity. It made him sound strong, straightforward.

The three trampolinists were a tall gangly West Indian girl called Kathryn, a stocky muscular fourteen-year-old called Markos, who looked Greek, and a petite fair-haired girl called Cherry. Kathryn, who had what Dan called a 'la-di-da' accent, hunched herself over as if trying to appear smaller, Cherry giggled a lot, and Markos stared at Stewart all the time frowning with concentration. Daniel immediately sensed an undercurrent of excitement.

Cherry was the first to get on to the trampoline.

'Cherry,' said Stewart, 'I know you have beautiful hair, but I told you, if you wear it loose like that you'll blind yourself. Anyone got an elastic band?'

Cherry stood in her neat pink shorts and matching T-shirt and stared at him in dismay. Even when she was horrified she still looked pretty, thought Daniel.

Stewart climbed up on to the trampoline and tied her hair back with the lace of a trainer. Mortified, she flung her hands over her face.

'I look awful,' she protested.

'You look lovely,' said Stewart, sliding neatly off the trampoline. 'And you know it.'

She giggled and began jumping up and down.

To Daniel's surprise she was completely graceless. As she soared in the air, her legs and arms flew in all directions. Even Daniel could see she was jumping too fast.

'Start from scratch,' said Stewart. 'Feet apart. Arms slightly raised beside you. Now bend your knees, push those heels into the webbing and jump. Bring your legs together and point your toes.'

She flung herself up but every time she landed it was in a different place. Now Daniel realised why they needed all sides covered.

'Remember,' Stewart shouted, 'when you see her coming towards you, don't step back. Step forward and push her back towards the centre.'

Tracking her, as she flew like a floppy rag doll in all directions, took all of Daniel's concentration. Eventually she managed to jump with her knees tucked up and later with her legs apart in a straddle. But as soon as she hit the trampoline she fell over.

'Good try, Cherry, but remember when you land, it's feet apart and bend your knees quickly.'

Flushed with tiredness, she nodded, sat on the edge and slid ungainly to the ground.

It was Markos' turn next.

'Wow!' Dan whispered, as Markos thumped his feet firmly into the canvas and soared into the air. He threw his legs well apart in a straddle, touching his toes. As soon as his feet hit the canvas he was up into a pike, legs drawn in front of him together, and touching his toes. Then to Dan's amazement he slammed his feet back into the canvas, and hardly had he left it than he drove his elbows down beside him and did a somersault, landing with precision on his feet.

Dan was about to yell out 'fantastic', when Stewart interrupted.

'Not bad, Markos. You have a good driving spin there, but it's a gymnastic somersault, not a trampoline one.'

He was criticizing him! Daniel was gobsmacked. He had just done a somersault and the man was criticizing him!

'Wally!' whispered Daniel crossly.

But Markos was standing with his powerful hands on his hips, nodding.

'I know,' he said. 'I'm so used to doing somersaults on a mat, I go into the old shoulders-down routine automatically.'

'What did he do wrong?' asked Daniel. 'It looked great to me.'

'When you do a somersault on the floor you need to drive your shoulders down really hard, whereas a lot of the things we do on the trampoline are based on hip movements, not shoulders. Here, I'll show you.'

Markos slipped off the trampoline to cover for Stewart.

'Now my hips will take me halfway through the somersault. Height first, hips back, then tuck. That's why we practise the tuck jump. It's good preparation for a somersault.'

Dan watched Stewart glide up into the air. At the height of his third jump, he jerked his hips back and tucked, and Dan could see what he meant. His somersault was nowhere near the canvas. He span at the height of the jump and then gracefully unfolded out of it, his body unbending, hips forward like a curved bow.

'Have another try,' he said swinging himself off the trampoline.

Markos bounced back on to the canvas.

'And let's see if you can straighten your knees and point your toes,' he added.

'I'm pointing them as hard as I can!'

'I know,' said Stewart smiling, 'and it shows. You have far more stretch than you had two months ago. We'll have those legs straight yet. Now wait till I tell you to turn.'

Markos began to thump his feet into the canvas again, soaring up again, a compact square of muscle, neat, feet together but knees still bent.

'Now!' yelled Stewart.

Markos bent his arms and whipped them down. He span and descended speedily in Daniel's direction. Daniel gritted his teeth and flung his arms out in front of him. Immediately Kathryn was by his side and in a second they had pushed Markos back to the centre.

Daniel watched mesmerised as Markos repeatedly grew worse and worse. So much for trampoline somersaults, he thought, glaring at Stewart.

'You're trying too hard,' said Stewart. 'You're putting enough energy in for a double, if not a triple somersault. Remember, hips, a quick tuck and unfold. Try counting "one".'

Markos nodded.

Daniel could see the intensity of Markos' concentration as he jumped powerfully down into the trampoline. He was convinced Stewart had got it all wrong. Perhaps he was jealous of Markos. But to Daniel's amazement, Markos showed respect for Stewart.

Markos was still jumping, still not attempting the somersault. What is he waiting for? thought Daniel, feeling tense with excitement. Then as Markos reached the top of the next jump, Daniel watched his hips jerk back and at the last moment he snapped in his knees, let them go instantly and arched his body as he descended. As his feet touched the canvas he bent his knees sharply and he was as solid as a rock.

To Daniel's surprise he found himself clapping along with Cherry and Kathryn.

'I got it!' Markos yelled.

'How did it feel?' asked Stewart.

'Weird. It really felt as if I wasn't trying hard enough. It's such a quick tuck!'

Stewart nodded. 'Like to try a swivel hips?'

Markos gave a loud groan and collapsed on to the canvas. 'Is this my reward?'

'Come on,' said Stewart. 'You conquered the single somersault.'

The swivel hips consisted of jumping into a sitting position called a seat drop, rising, doing half a turn, sitting on the other side and bouncing back on to the feet.

Markos managed to do the 'seat drop' but instead of swivelling he tucked up his knees and kept trying to go sideways into the second seat drop.

'Sorry, but it's just not going in,' said Markos sitting on the canvas.

'Let's get back to basics,' suggested Stewart. 'Do a seat drop into a front drop. That will get you used to swinging your legs underneath you.'

Markos scrambled back up to his feet. He was about to begin thumping into the canvas when Stewart stopped him.

'Do it from standing. You don't need so much height.'

Markos stood with his legs apart, threw himself into a seat drop and as he rose into the air from it, he drew his legs back underneath him, landed full length on to his front and back on to his feet.

'There, not so bad was it?' exclaimed Stewart. 'Now remember the feeling of your legs swinging underneath you, but keep straight and add a half turn into a seat drop the other side.'

Markos tried but instead of adding the half turn he kept

bringing his knees up into a tuck and falling over.

After a few more turns, Stewart suggested he take a break and have another crack at it later.

It was Kathryn's turn next. As she hauled her long lean limbs clumsily on to the trampoline, she gave the appearance of a dark brown spider.

She was wearing tight-fitting black Bermuda shorts, which reminded Daniel of his mother's rowing shorts, and a brightly-coloured vest in orange and black. To Daniel's amazement, as soon as she began jumping, she seemed to elongate out like a stretched rubber band.

Taking her time, her legs straight and pointed, she soared upwards like an arrow. She waited until she was at the height of her jump before she did a straddle or a pike jump and it was breathtakingly beautiful to watch.

She then jumped into a seat drop, her feet so pointed, her legs so straight you could have put a ruler across them. As she rose back into the air she drew her legs underneath her, twisted as though twisting a hoola hoop round her waist and landed in a seat drop on the other side.

Daniel clapped and then suddenly felt self-conscious. Stewart was smiling at him.

'Yes,' he agreed. 'That's how a swivel hips should look.'

Daniel glanced over at Cherry and Markos to see if they were jealous but they were too absorbed in watching her. There was a really good feeling of support around the trampoline. So much so, that he suddenly wanted to be up there jumping too. Meanwhile, he watched Kathryn soaring gracefully and powerfully to a tremendous height. Suddenly she did a single somersault, unfolded out of it and to Daniel's horror appeared to be falling on her way down. Instead she landed in a front drop, tucked up round to another front drop on the other side and was back on to her feet again.

Daniel was so absorbed in watching her, that Stewart had to speak several times to him before his question finally penetrated.

'Me?' he exclaimed. 'Up there?'

'If you want.'

He looked at the others. 'Won't they mind?'

But he could see by their shaking heads that they didn't.

'You won't be doing somersaults today though.'

Daniel laughed, and it shook him by its unfamiliarity. It was then that he realised he hadn't laughed for a very long time. He didn't even get uptight when he couldn't get on to the trampoline. Markos came round and cupped his hands into a step for him. And Daniel collapsed laughing again as he sprawled spread-eagled on to the canvas.

'When you've recovered,' said Stewart, 'start by just jumping on the canvas. Get used to the feel of it. It's springier than some trampolines, being webbed, and you'd better do it in your socks.'

Daniel threw his trainers on to the floor, bent his knees and dug his heels into the canvas.

* * *

94

'You're quick,' said Stewart, surprised. 'Have you done anything like this before?'

'No,' said Daniel.

'Gymnastics?'

'No.'

'You can point your feet as well as Kathryn.'

Daniel could feel himself beginning to blush. He prayed he wouldn't be asked any more questions. 'I've dived a bit,' he said hurriedly.

'Like to have a go at the swivel hips?' Stewart asked.

'Yeah!'

The others laughed at his eagerness.

'Now remember, swing your legs underneath you as you rise.'

Daniel nodded.

He stood with his legs apart, feet parallel on the webbed canvas and pushed off into a seat drop. Then with all the strength he could muster he swung his legs underneath him.

'Turn!' yelled Stewart.

The next thing he knew he was facing the other side but on his back. He was just about to curse when to his surprise he heard the others clapping.

'That's a great start!' said Stewart.

'Really?' said Daniel, hauling himself up to his feet.

'Again?' asked Stewart.

Daniel grinned. He stood with his feet apart again, raised his arms and pushed himself up into the air.

* * *

After they had folded the trampoline and wheeled it back against one of the walls in the gym, Markos and Cherry went off into a corner and chatted. One of Daniel's trainers had landed by a crimson tracksuit. He found that he and Kathryn were heading in the same direction.

As he pulled on his shoes, he watched her hauling on the tracksuit trousers out of the corner of his eye and he suddenly felt shy.

'You're good,' he blurted out.

She looked down at him and beamed. 'Thanks.'

She sat beside him and pulled on her shoes.

'You don't do yoga by any chance?' he added casually.

'No.' She looked hesitant for a moment. 'If I tell you something will you promise to keep quiet about it?'

'Yeah. Course.'

'I do ballet,' she whispered.

'What's wrong with that?' he asked surprised.

'Look at the height of me. I'm only eleven and I'm still growing. My mother's convinced I'll be nearly two metres by the time I've finished. Can you imagine what people would think of a beanpole like me doing ballet! They'd laugh their heads off.'

'Is that why you hunch yourself over?'

'Do I?'

He nodded. 'Except when you're on the trampoline and then you look really graceful.'

She gave a bashful smile.

'Actually,' he said slowly, 'I have a secret to confess too.'

'You do ballet too?'

'Much worse. My dad calls me and Mum cranky. He says we'll be turning vegetarian next.'

'Why?'

'Because we . . .' he paused. 'Are you ready for this?'

'Yes,' she said impatiently. 'Go on.'

'We do yoga.'

'Oh. So that's why you thought I did it.'

'Yes. Don't tell anyone. I'm only supposed to do it in secret at my mum's. My dad hates it. He says if I ever do it in public or in front of any of his rugby-loving friends, he'll pretend he doesn't know me.'

'I'm afraid I don't know much about yoga.'

'I'll show you a lotus position.'

He gave a quick look round but the hall was empty. He sat cross-legged and folded his feet over the opposite thighs.

'Doesn't that hurt?' she gasped.

'No. You have to work up to it though.'

'But how did you start it if your dad . . .'

'I didn't. My mum started doing it first, three years ago, for her nerves.'

'Did it work?'

'Yes. She stopped moaning and started getting more confident. Only snag was she got so confident she asked my dad for a divorce, and I took it up for *my* nerves!'

Kathryn laughed. She grabbed her tracksuit top. 'I'm going upstairs for a snack. Want to come?'

Daniel hesitated for a moment. His dad might worry if he was late. He smiled. So what! Let him have a taste of his own medicine. 'Yeah,' he said. 'Why not?'

His father's flat was only five flights of stairs up, but to his annoyance, he had found himself leaping up the stairs two at a time, instead of walking. He stopped for a moment to catch his breath and wipe the sweat from his face. He didn't want to look exhausted when he made his entrance.

As soon as he reached the fifth-floor landing, he noticed that the door was ajar. He hesitated, alarmed. Perhaps there had been a break-in. Perhaps his father was lying in a pool of blood, bound and gagged on the sitting room floor. That would explain why he hadn't arrived at the Leisure Centre.

Cautiously he sidled towards the door and pushed it open.

Scattered across the tiny hallway were suitcases, newspapers and chairs. The place had been ransacked. He felt sick. 'Dad,' he called out shakily.

There was no answer. From behind the closed sitting room door he heard the sounds of a television.

'Dad,' he began again.

A loud yell came from behind the door. 'Stop him you silly . . .' It was him.

'Oh no,' yelled a second voice.

Furious, Daniel threw open the sitting room door with

such ferocity that the door knob hit the wall.

His father was sitting on the settee staring at the box. Another man Daniel didn't know was sitting in the nearby armchair. By their feet was a row of empty beer cans.

'Hi, Titch,' said his father cheerfully over his shoulder. 'Good to see you!'

Daniel strode angrily across the room and stood in front of the screen.

'Hey, Titch, stop larking about,' protested his father.

'Dad, you were supposed to meet me at the Leisure Centre. Remember?'

'Sorry mate, I completely forgot Trev was coming round. I left a message to say forget about the swimming and come round and watch this.'

Daniel turned. 'Rugby? In the summer!' he exclaimed. 'Wait a minute. You've seen this match before.'

'I know. It's so fantastic. You'll learn a lot from these players. Trev brought it round on his video. Good of him, wasn't it?'

Daniel glanced briefly at the man in the armchair. The man gave him a cheery wave. With their beer bellies, he and his dad looked like Tweedledee and Tweedledum.

'You could have watched this later,' Daniel said pointedly.

'Trev was only here for the afternoon. I knew you'd understand.'

'I don't, Dad.'

'Hey, you're not upset, are you?'

'I'm angry, Dad.'

'Titch,' he said quietly. 'We have a guest.'

'My name is Dan. I'm not going to answer to Titch any more.'

'All right, your name is not Titch. Look, I'm sorry. Now if you don't mind,' he indicated the set.

'Did your guest know you were supposed to meet me?'

'Yes, but I told him you'd understand when you got the message.'

'I didn't get the message.'

'That's not my fault, is it? Why didn't you phone?'

'Because . . .' he felt lost for words. 'You still should have come!'

'Come on, Titch . . .'

With that Daniel turned off the set.

A flush of colour swept across his father's face. 'You've gone too far,' he began.

'I want an apology.'

'You've had it. How many more times do I have to say I'm sorry?'

Daniel switched on the set and stormed out of the room. He heard his father rewind the video. 'Kids!' he heard him mutter to his friend. 'I left a message. What more could I do?'

Daniel opened the kitchen door. Seven days ago, he had scrubbed and washed the kitchen and helped his dad move in. He had been so angry with his mother for not helping out that they had had a major quarrel. When finally he had yelled, 'But why not?' she had just answered quietly, 'Because it's just a waste of time.'

Now tins of every variety surrounded the overflowing rubbish bin which was leaning precariously against the sink unit. Stacked high in the washing-up bowl and on the draining board was a week's worth of unwashed crockery.

He stared stunned at the filthy floor. It wasn't just the disbelief that his father could live like this, he just couldn't work out how mud could reach a fifth-floor flat.

He backed into the corridor and climbed over the suitcases and newspapers towards his bedroom.

The door was stuck. He leaned against it, thrust his arm round and grabbed a holdall, pushing it and a towel to one side. The door fell open.

It was only too obvious that his father had been using the room as a dumping ground.

'It's only temporary,' he said, mimicking his father's jovial voice. But then any mess he made always was 'only temporary'.

For a moment he stood in the debris, too numbed with disappointment and hurt to move. There was no sign of his bed. Like the floor, it was submerged under a mountain of shoes, magazines, boxes, tools and bulging bin-liners.

It was all over. He had been defeated. There was no way his parents would ever get back together again now. His mother wouldn't want to give up her rowing and training sessions to restart cleaning up after his dad. And however much Daniel tried to help him, his dad would never change. In fact, he had grown worse.

As he gazed at the mess, feeling thoroughly depressed, he was suddenly conscious of a sense of relief.

'That's it!' he muttered angrily. 'From now on I'll please myself. They'll just have to sort out their own problems.' And with that he picked up two bin bags and hurled them determinedly off the bed.

Later, in the kitchen, while the kettle was boiling, Daniel wiped some tomato sauce from the telephone receiver and dialled. His mother must have been waiting for him. The phone was picked up instantly.

'Mum, I've changed my mind about tomorrow. I'd like to have a crack at the rowing.'

There was silence.

'Mum?'

'He didn't turn up, did he?' she said at last.

'No.'

He heard her sigh. 'I'm sorry, love.'

'It's OK, I had a fantastic time. I went on a trampoline.'

'On your own?'

'No. There was a coach there. He said I'm good.'

'Great!'

'And I met this girl there called Kathryn. We went to the canteen afterwards and it turns out she's starting at Royston Road next term too.'

'Every cloud has a silver lining, eh?'

'Sort of.'

'Have you told Dad?'

'No. He's busy.'

'Watching *Grandstand?*'

'No. Rugby. It's a video.'

'Oh.' There was a brief pause. 'I'll pick you up about nine-thirty then.'

'Do you mind if I pop round for breakfast?'

'No. I'll come round about eight then, shall I?'

'No. I can walk.'

'Are you sure?'

'Mum, it's only three streets away.'

'Do you want me to drop you at Dad's after the rowing?'

'I'll see how I feel.'

'Don't take it to heart. Your dad doesn't mean to hurt you.'

'I know. Mum?'

'Yes.'

'There's something I want to say.'

'Yes?'

'It's about rugby.'

'Oh.'

'No, listen.' He took a deep breath. 'I want you to know that if I ever do decide to play rugby, it won't be because I'm trying to please Dad and it won't be because you don't like macho games and I'm trying to get up your nose. It'll be because I want to do it. OK?'

'Fine. As long as you clean your muddy boots and wash your kit.'

He laughed. That was typical of his mother now.

'*Do* you want to play rugby?' she asked hesitantly.

'Not now. But I might later. Who knows?' He paused. 'There's something else too. Don't introduce me as Titch tomorrow, will you? I don't want to be called that any more.'

'I never do anyway.'

With a surprise he realised it was true. He had spent so much time trying to get his father's attention that he had hardly noticed what his mother said or did.

'Why don't you, Mum?'

'You don't seem small to me.'

'But I am.'

'Well, if I got out a tape measure. Yes. Probably. But you're so packed with energy, you've always seemed on the big side.'

He smiled. 'Thanks, Mum.'

He made three mugs of tea, took them into the sitting room and handed one to Trev.

'Thanks, Dan,' he said.

He gave a mug to his father.

'All right now?' asked his dad.

Daniel nodded and sat beside him on the settee.

His father raised his mug. 'Cheers, then.'

'Cheers,' said Daniel, and he sat back, drew up his legs and watched rugby league in the lotus position.

The Smile

'Waaagh!'

'Not *again*,' Josh moaned.

He switched on his torch to look at his bedside clock.

It was twenty-past four.

He dragged his bedding up over his head but his baby brother's howls pierced through his bedroom wall and penetrated every duck feather in his duvet.

It had taken Josh nearly an hour to drift back to sleep after the last bout of wailing. He groaned. This was what torturers did when they wanted to extract vital information from their victims. Sleep deprivation they called it. Josh would have told anybody anything a long time ago.

The torturer in Josh's case was only seventeen days old. If Josh didn't get some peace soon, he thought grimly, his brother would be lucky to live through his eighteenth day.

He stuck his nose out.

It was still as black as pitch outside.

The bedroom door next to his room opened. The howl rose in crescendo and then faded as the door closed. He heard his father padding quietly along the landing to the bathroom. He was on the morning shift that week; his first one back to work after the baby's birth.

Josh wanted to join him for a chat but he knew his father left getting up to the last minute so that he could have an extra five minutes sleep. Not that he had had much chance of that with the howler. For three hours, Josh had listened to his parents taking turns with Michael, walking up and down the creaking floorboards, singing to him, talking to him, but making no headway.

Finally, in desperation, they had started yelling at one another, blaming each other for the baby being awake. And his mother had shouted, 'Look at us! We're rowing in front of him. I never wanted to do that!'

Then Josh had heard his father interrupt her and tell her to look at Michael.

There was silence.

Their row had sent him to sleep.

'We'll have to think of something new to argue about the next time he won't stop crying,' his father had said. And his mother had burst out laughing.

Shivering outside their bedroom door eavesdropping, Josh felt cut off from their secret world. There they were the three of them, wrapped up together while he lay alone in the next room, forgotten.

He heard the front door close and suddenly the house was silent.

'At last,' he muttered, 'I can get to sleep.'

He closed his eyes but they sprang back open. Now it was the wallpaper which kept him awake. Even in the dark he could still make out the large orange and purple flowers which ran amok over every available inch on the wall.

His parents had promised they would decorate his room, but when? His howling brother took up so much of their time they didn't even have time to talk to him, let alone start stripping walls.

They hadn't even put up curtains for him.

He glared in the dark at the wooden boxes balanced on top of one another in an alcove. They were crammed with comics and books. Josh kept his clothes in open suitcases and a holdall on the floor and used the rail in the cupboard for his string puppets.

He didn't really mind the clutter. It was the wallpaper which made it unbearable. It must have been chosen by someone who was colour-blind and short-sighted. Every time Josh entered the room he wanted to put a paper bag over his head.

His parents ignored his pleas for mercy. They were too wrapped up in talking about the coming baby.

In desperation, he had worn sunglasses in bed to make the point but his mother thought he was just trying to be cool and his father was so busy working on the kitchen ready for the onslaught of Babygros that he didn't even notice.

That was another thing Josh resented. The move. His parents said they needed more space with the baby coming so Josh had to leave the street he had lived in for as long as he could remember and the room which was *him*. And to cap it all, his beloved brother decided to be born the day before his tenth birthday which meant his party was cancelled. Even his puppet theatre was still stuck in the bottom of a trunk. And all because of his wonderful new brother.

'Do you realise,' he had said to his mother the previous night, 'do you realise he'll be with us for *years!*'

And his mother had beamed and said, 'Yes.'

She'd tried to persuade him to help look after him but he wasn't interested. He was still too angry with him for ruining his birthday party, ruining his entire life in fact.

'Silence,' he whispered to the hideous flowers on the wall. 'Wonderful silence!'

He closed his eyes again.

It was no good. He had to find out why it was so quiet.

His mother was sitting propped up by pillows on the mattress, which was on the carpet. Michael's Moses basket stood on a trunk at the end of it. It was empty. It didn't take long for Josh to find out what had caused the silence. His mother was feeding *him*.

She looked up at Josh and smiled. Her face was still pale and the bags under her eyes looked even darker but she looked so happy that she could have been a lighthouse.

A red hand-towel was draped over the lampshade next to her to help soften the light.

Coming from the cold landing the warm air nearly knocked him over. It was like the hot house in Kew Gardens. It was kept at that temperature for Michael.

'Did he wake you again?' his mother asked. Josh nodded and ambled towards the bed.

'Come on,' she said, indicating the pillows beside her. He climbed in next to her.

She leaned her head against his shoulder. 'Sorry I can't give you a hug. My hands are full.'

'I can see,' he grunted.

He glanced at the tiny baby lying on a pillow on his mother's lap.

He'd been embarrassed the first time he had seen her breast-feeding him but now he was so used to it, the sight was like wallpaper. Nice wallpaper.

'You were like this once,' she murmured.

'M'm,' he said, disbelieving he could be quite so helpless. 'You always seem to be feeding him.'

'His stomach is so tiny he can only take it in small doses and he's also learning to suck. There's a lot for him to take in and learn.'

'I know.'

He gave a weary sigh.

'The first month is always the worst,' she reassured him. 'After that it gets better. He'll be more settled and . . .'

'A month!'

A month of this and he'd be a wreck.

'Poor thing. Why don't you bring a sleeping bag in here if you get lonely?'

'I might as well. I can hear him every time he cries. Do I have to go to school today?'

'Not if you don't feel like it. I can send a note explaining.'

'But Dad's gone to work, hasn't he?'

'Yes.'

'Then I suppose I'd better go. It's just I'd like to get some sleep.'

'Wouldn't we all.'

He gazed round at all the congratulations cards. They covered the tops of three chests of drawers. Bouquets of flowers drooped in vases in amongst them and on the floor.

'How long will you keep the cards and flowers?' he asked.

'I don't know. I still like seeing them. And, anyway, clearing them away isn't high on my list of priorities at the moment.'

Like my bedroom walls, he thought.

They fell silent and watched the baby sucking.

When Josh woke two hours later, his mother had only just finished feeding Michael. She had propped him into a sitting position and was supporting his tiny floppy body with one hand and gently tapping his back with the other. He seemed to be staring at Josh. He gave a deep burp.

Josh smiled and his mother saw him and it annoyed him to be caught out. But it was funny that such a loud sound could come from someone so small. Even his farts seemed to shake his Moses basket. Sometimes he woke himself up with them.

Outside, the dawn was beginning to lighten the sky.

'Josh,' said his mother slowly, 'would you mind holding Michael while I take a bath?'

'Oh, Mum,' he began.

'Please. This may be my only chance before Dad gets home and then he'll be cooking the meal.'

He gave a resigned sigh.

'Thanks,' she said.

She helped him plump the pillows up behind him and refused to hand Michael over until Josh had convinced her he was comfortable. He leaned back, crossed his legs and placed a pillow over his knees. She placed the baby on top of it.

'He won't wet me, will he?'

'I can't promise,' she said, 'but I doubt it. And anyway he'll wet the pillow, won't he?'

'I suppose so.'

She ruffled Josh's springy hair.

'I won't be long. I'll turn the light off so he can doze off more easily.'

He was still staring solemnly at Josh. A slow trickle of milk escaped from the corner of his mouth. His mother dabbed at it with a tissue. She kissed Josh on the cheek.

'Oh, Mum,' he protested, 'don't be so soppy.'

She laughed.

Josh watched her stagger blearily to the door. She had probably had less sleep than all of them. He suddenly felt ashamed at being so grumpy.

He looked round at the cluttered room. The curtains had been drawn open. A street light lit the stripped branches of a tree on the opposite side of the road. Occasionally he heard a car drive past but aside from that it was quiet. It seemed that everyone in the street was asleep apart from his family.

It all seemed unreal to be sitting sweating in his T-shirt when he could see the pink of a winter dawn suffusing the sky. It had started to snow. Flakes of it floated and drifted past the window, feathery, landing on the branches and melting.

He looked down at his seventeen-day-old brother as he lay in the crook of his left arm. He was still staring at Josh and frowning.

Josh swallowed. He had dreaded being left alone with him and now here he was, stuck with him. He cleared his throat. 'I'm your brother,' he explained awkwardly.

It was such a penetrating stare that it made Josh feel uncomfortable. And he didn't like the frown. Frowns meant worry. What did a seventeen-day-old baby have to worry about?

He let his fingers glide across the frown, up from the bridge of his small round nose, fanning outwards above his eyebrows to the dark hair which plastered his head.

'There,' he said quietly, 'I'll stroke that old frown away.'

It was something to do, he told himself. It would stop him getting bored. But the more he stroked, the more absorbed he grew in his task.

Gradually the frown lifted and dissolved under his fingertips. As his brother's forehead smoothed out, his eyelids lowered.

And then it happened. Quick. Fleeting. But it happened and he alone saw it. And it wasn't caused by wind because he had already burped.

A smile. A blissful contented smile. Not crooked but both corners of his mouth curving gently upward. And then it was gone and his brother was in a deep sleep.

In that instant, Josh was filled with a passion for his brother so intense that it brought a lump to his throat. Suddenly, sleepless nights were of no importance. From the moment he had glimpsed his smile, he vowed he would care for him. No one but no one would lay one finger on him. If anyone dared hurt him he would pulverise them. If he was in danger he'd rescue him. He would dive into icy waters to save him. He would climb mountains. He'd swing from the trees! He'd . . .

And then his brother farted and opened his eyes for a fraction before falling back to sleep again.

Josh laughed.

That'll teach me to get soppy, he thought. But he still couldn't take his eyes off him. 'Tomorrow,' he whispered,

'I'll unpack my puppet theatre. For when you're older.'

Outside the snow continued to fall and Josh smiled. He smiled so wide that his cheeks ached and so deep that he forgot about clocks and cancelled birthday parties and purple and orange wallpaper.

He had something far far better to think about now. He had Michael.

Beginners

The scene was over. The stage was plunged into black-out. Tony turned swiftly and headed for the nearest opening in the wings, aiming for a strip of white tape which had been stuck on the wooden floor.

One of the actors ran past him and flung back the door leading to the corridor. For a brief moment, a shaft of light exposed Tony's mother who was standing, waiting for him.

Tony stopped at the tape and stared down at it, ashamed. He was so appalled by what he had done on stage that he was certain he would never be allowed into a theatre again. He glanced sideways at the prompt corner. Sue, the deputy stage manager, was perched on the high stool, leaning over the prompt book and giving a lighting cue into a small microphone. He didn't know whether to thank, apologise or curse her.

He took a step, hesitated, and then stumbled back towards his mother.

She swung back the door to the corridor and put her arm round his shoulders, but he couldn't bring himself to look at her. A deep ache welled up into his throat causing his nose and eyes to sting fiercely.

One of the actors strode past them, a shabby duffel coat over his faded corduroys. He was playing the Social Worker in the next scene.

'You handled that prompt well,' he remarked. Tony whipped his head round but he had already disappeared into the wings.

He had forgotten that the play was relayed backstage over the Tannoy system. That meant the rest of the cast must have heard him being prompted from their dressing rooms.

His mother gave him a squeeze. 'Come on, love,' she murmured. 'Let's get back to the dressing-room.'

He walked beside her, his hands shoved in his pockets. And still he wouldn't look at her. He couldn't. And, anyway, she wouldn't understand. Not like Brian's mother.

They turned up the curved stone steps which led to his dressing-room – the dressing-room he shared with Annie. He couldn't be in one of the men's dressing-rooms because his mother had to remain with him. She was employed as the theatre chaperone for both him and Brian. They had to have one. It was the law. And it was the law that he was only allowed to do so many performances a week, which was why the theatre had to have two boys playing the same part on alternate nights.

His mother pushed open a door off the first landing. Tony paused for a moment in the doorway and took in the two mirrors on the far wall surrounded with lighted bulbs and 'good luck' cards, the table with make-up and tissues spread out on it, the small chipped sink in the corner, the old threadbare armchair, the tatty rug on the floor, the rail with his and Annie's change of clothes hanging from it.

Annie had explained how the lights around the mirrors gave an idea of how one's make-up would look under stage lighting. Tony didn't need much make-up, just some base and a bit of mascara because his lashes were so fair, but halfway through the play he had to look as though he hadn't had much sleep. Arthur, who had been fifty years in the theatre, had shown him how to make up a mixture of greasepaint in the palm of his hand so that he could thumb-in shadows under his eyes.

As he gazed at the greasepaint sticks, Arthur had lent him, he remembered what he had done. How could he face Arthur now?

He walked towards his dressing-table pulling off his sweater, and sank into the chair.

'You'd better get changed,' said his mother.

He raised his head and looked at her in the mirror. She was holding out a school uniform.

'Yeah,' he said dismally.

He took it from her and slung the blazer over the back of the chair.

Feeling a mixture of numbness and pain, he slipped on the grey shirt and knotted the stripy tie. He kicked off his sneakers, unzipped his jeans and stepped into the long grey flannels. Before he could swallow the tears back, they rushed down his face. He brushed them aside angrily and sat down to put on his lace-ups.

His mother drew up her chair beside him. 'Don't take it to heart, love. There's other nights.'

'I've only got four performances to go.'

He tugged hard at the laces, blinking away the blur in his eyes.

'I don't understand what happened. It was only when I saw everyone staring at me that I realised it was my turn to speak. And then I went completely blank. Even after I'd been prompted I forgot how to do it. It felt like I was improvising. It was a shambles.'

'It sounded fine. Funnily enough, it sounded better.'

'How could it?' he muttered. He shook his head. 'Now they'll never ask me to work here again. It'd be all right if there weren't two of us playing the same part. It's not fair. Brian gets all this extra help.'

His mother gave a sigh. They had been through this discussion before. Many times. She picked up a bundle of knitting from the corner of the table and sat back.

'Why won't you help me?' he asked.

'I've told you. I'm not a director.'

'Neither is Brian's mum and she coaches him before every single performance.'

'I test your lines, don't I?'

'Yes, but you don't tell me how to say them.'

'That's the director's job.'

'But he never tells me either. He just talks about what kind of boy Andrew is, and his feelings, and that I just need to listen to the others and then reply. When I try and put in a gesture like Brian, he tells me not to do it. That's what mucked everything up tonight.'

His mother lowered her knitting.

'What do you mean?'

'I did this arm movement Brian's just put in. It completely threw me.'

'You were trying to copy Brian?'

'Yes.'

'But why?'

'He and his mother know more about the theatre than I do, so he must be doing it better.'

'Don't be daft. You were picked at the audition, same as him.'

He swung round.

'Mum, be honest. Do you think I got the part just because I'm small?'

'There were plenty other small ones there.'

'But most of them were eleven, like the character.'

'There were other thirteen year olds too,' she pointed out. 'You got picked because you were good enough. Now tie your other shoe-lace up.'

He bent over and tightened it. He wished he could

believe her, but she didn't know anything about acting and the theatre. All she seemed to care about was the money angle. He remembered with embarrassment how she had written off to some place in London as soon as he'd been offered the part, and the next thing he knew, she'd asked the Management to pay him and Brian more money. He nearly died, especially when Brian's mother said she didn't want anything to do with it, and that Brian would be only too glad to have the honour of performing in this new play for nothing. He had gone through agonies while the Management were making their decision, terrified he would lose the part.

There was a knock at the door.

He straightened up quickly.

It was Graham and Arthur. Tony reddened.

'Thought we'd pop in to see you,' said Graham. 'Heard you looked a bit down.'

'Yeah,' whispered Tony, glancing down at his hands.

'It's not because you dried, is it, old fellow?' boomed Arthur.

He nodded.

'Join the club,' said Graham. 'We've all done that.'

Tony looked up.

'Oh, yes,' added Arthur, 'me too.'

They came into the dressing-room. Arthur sat in the armchair and leaned forward intently, his hands clasped.

'I'm afraid we weren't much help,' he commented.

'Usually someone can feed you a line,' said Graham,

'but everything you were saying was supposed to be a revelation. And we all had to be dumbstruck.'

'Arthur, have you really dried too?'

'Worse. When I started out in weekly rep I was once playing two characters in the same play, and was so tired one night that I did my quick change too soon. I was just about to rush on when I realised I was the wrong person. It was too late to change back so I had to stand in the wings and listen to my fellow actors having to make up the rest of the scene without me.'

At that moment, Sue's voice came over the Tannoy. 'Mr Henderson and Mr Forsyth, this is your call, your call please, Mr Henderson and Mr Forsyth. Thank you.'

They leapt to their feet and made for the door. Just as Arthur was about to close it, he turned.

'By the way, old boy, I rather like the way you did the scene after that dry. More real.'

Tony stared after him, open-mouthed.

His mother smiled.

'There you are,' she said casually. 'They don't think badly of you.'

Tony listened to the Tannoy. The scene between the character Annie was playing and one of the people in the communal house was coming to an end.

He slipped on the school blazer. Annie would have walked off the set by now. She'd be hurrying into the wings and making for the corridor.

He sat on the edge of his chair and stared at the door in the mirror. As soon as he heard her running up the stairs he began to sweat.

His mother, observing him, said nothing.

Suddenly the door burst open and Annie rushed in, pulling off her jersey at the same time.

Tony looked away.

He was still smarting from the telling-off she had given him the previous week, when he had tried to tell her a joke just as she was about to go on stage. But he hadn't meant to upset her. On the contrary, he wanted to impress her. 'Never, never do that again,' she had raged. 'The time in the wings is preparation time. You're working with a professional company now. I expect you to behave like a professional.'

Now he took a deep breath.

'Sorry about the prompt,' he blurted out.

'You handled it like a pro,' she remarked.

Tony whirled round.

She had changed into the baggy green trousers and voluminous red sweater ready for their last scene together. He watched her tuck her long auburn hair into a short wig.

'Aren't you angry?'

She separated a grip with her teeth and slid it in behind one ear.

'No. It's an awful thing to happen to anyone.'

'But everyone in the audience must have heard it.'

She sat back and looked at him. 'But you didn't fall apart at the seams. You picked it up and carried on as though nothing had happened.'

'I had to. It's an important scene.'

'Yes. You cared more about saving the scene than nursing your own bruised ego.'

'What's an ego?'

She laughed. 'You'll find out soon enough if you stay in this business.'

'You mean you think I might be good enough to be a professional actor one day?'

She touched his arm. 'Is that what you want?'

He blushed. 'More than anything else in the world.'

'Oh dear. You have got it badly.'

'You make it sound like a disease.'

'It is.'

She let go of his arm and applied some fresh lipstick to her mouth.

'Do you think,' he began hesitantly, 'I'm as good as Brian?'

She looked quizzically at him.

'He really worries you, doesn't he?'

'Yes.'

'Just because he gives a different performance it doesn't make his better or worse. You're different people. You couldn't possibly play it the same way.'

'But he's so good technically. I mean his mother is always helping and . . .' He stopped.

The two women glanced at one another.

Annie turned back to the mirror, smacked her lips together and tissued off a smudge.

'Yes. Brian has quite a problem there,' she muttered.

Tony stared at her.

'A problem? But she helps him.'

'She hinders him, Tony.'

'But he was word-perfect on the first day of rehearsal. Not like me.'

'Or me,' she reminded him. 'Or Arthur, or anyone else. We learnt our lines as we rehearsed the play. Acting is about working with other people, not doing a solo spot with them.'

'But he says his lines so clearly and makes fantastic gestures.'

She turned to face him.

'Tony, I know technique is important. I mean, if a deaf old lady has paid for a ticket at the back of the theatre she wants to be able to hear what's going on. But if there's no heart . . .' She paused. 'I'm not saying Brian has no heart, but when he's on stage with me I feel his mother's with us too. I can see him desperately trying to remember her latest instruction. His eyes glaze over as though he's reading a manual inside his head. Sometimes it's so bad I can't even make eye-contact with him. It's terrifying for him. She really winds him up. I'm only thankful she's not allowed backstage during the performance.'

'I thought it was a rule that no one was allowed.'

'It is. But his mother was hoping to be the chaperone on his performance nights. We soon put a stop to that.'

Tony was flabbergasted.

'What do you mean?'

'We all got together and begged the director not to allow it. Luckily for us, your mother agreed to be one for both of you.'

'Mum! You never said.'

'And a bloody good chaperone she is too,' continued Annie. 'He's a bag of nerves when he arrives. At least the poor little bugger has thirty-five minutes peace before curtain up. It takes all that time for your mother to calm him down.'

Tony turned to his mother.

'Why didn't you tell me?'

'I was afraid it might get back to Brian. It'd upset him if he knew people weren't too fond of her. You won't say anything, will you?'

He shook his head.

'I thought you were doing the extra chaperoning for the money. I thought you were doing everything for the money.' He paused. 'Like all that stuff about my wages.'

'Have you heard yet?' asked Annie.

Tony's mother nodded.

'Perhaps tonight would be a good time to tell him.'

'What's going on?' said Tony, eyeing them suspiciously.

His mother drew out a piece of paper from her handbag. It was a typed form.

Below the words British Actors' Equity Association was written APPLICATION FOR CHILDREN'S TEMPORARY MEMBERSHIP. His mother had filled in his name and address and the repertory theatre and production underneath.

'I didn't want to say anything till it had arrived. I had to send off a copy of the contract to London first. 'That's why I asked them to raise your pay. If you earn half of what the adults get, you can apply for child membership. It's only temporary, but if you do any other acting jobs in the next few years then, when you're sixteen, you can try and get something called your provisional card. It's ever so hard to get that one and you can't get work without it, so . . .'

'You mean I'm sort of a Junior member of the Actors' Union?'

'If you want to be. If you sign this form. It's up to you.'

'Oh Mum,' he breathed.

'I'm not pushing you to be an actor, don't think that. But if later on that's still what you want, then there's no harm in helping things along a bit.'

Tony sat back and grinned.

'Got a biro?'

Annie picked one up from her dressing-table and handed it to him.

'Sure you know what you're doing?' she asked wryly.

He nodded happily.

Below where he was supposed to sign was another dotted line for the signature of a parent or guardian. Tony scribbled his name above it and slid the form towards his mother.

'Your turn now, Mum.'

'There,' she said, after signing it. 'I'll put it in the post tomorrow.'

Annie stood up and took an old raincoat from the rail.

'By the way,' she said, 'I know you dried in that scene, but afterwards, it was the best you'd ever played it. What happened?'

'That's what Arthur said!'

He caught sight of his mother suppressing a smile. 'And Mum.'

Just then Sue's voice came softly over the Tannoy. 'Ms Masterson and Mr Wilson, this is your call, your call please, Ms Masterson and Mr Wilson. 'Thank you.'

'Let's go,' said Annie.

As the three of them walked down the steps together, Tony turned over Annie's question in his mind. What *had* happened to him in that scene which had made it so different? Then it clicked. Usually he was always criticizing himself from outside, conscious of what he was doing with his arms and his voice. After he had been prompted he had thrown himself totally into the scene. And he had *believed* in what was happening! That was the difference.

They stepped through the door into the wings. He and Annie walked to the back, out of sight of the prompt corner. On the floor beside a makeshift gate was a wooden cue-board with two small red and green light bulbs on it.

In the shadows Tony gazed at Annie. Already she had started to look different. And then she wasn't Annie any more. She was Gwen Simpson, the single woman in her thirties who had moved out of the communal house where she had been living, because some of the house members had vetoed a child living in their communal set-up.

And he was Andrew, the eleven-year-old boy who was only meant to have stayed with her for a fortnight while his parents went away for a holiday – a holiday from which they never returned.

He could feel the tension leaving his body, and in its place, exhilaration.

The lights dimmed. The stage crew changed the set to a sparsely furnished sitting-room. The red 'warn' light came on for Annie. She raised the collar of her raincoat and picked up the bags of shopping which had been set there for her.

One of the assistant stage managers, a young man, stood by the gate. The green light flashed. He opened and slammed the gate, and Annie stepped on to a makeshift gravel path which led to the porch.

The red light was on for Tony's entrance. There was a sound of heavy rain. The assistant stage manager pumped water through a punctured hose which had been attached above a window, so that on stage it looked as though the rain was trickling down the glass.

128

Tony picked up his duffel bag, and the assistant stage manager sprayed his face with water.

The green light flashed on.

Tony slammed the gate and ran like fury up the path.

Black-out. He and Annie dashed into the wings. Behind thcm the lights came up again for a curtain call. Covered in custard and mashed potato and soaked from a water fight, they laughed at one another.

'That's the best we've ever done it!' panted Annie.

'It was fantastic!' he cried.

'*You* were fantastic. What happened?'

'I suddenly realised what the director was going on about. That they'd had to keep everything bottled up for months and they didn't have to do it any more because they had a place of their own. They didn't have to hold it all in till the next house meeting. They could just go mad.'

'You enjoyed smashing all that china tonight, didn't you?'

'Yeah.'

'Me too.'

She glanced on stage.

'Come on, it's our turn now.'

The rest of the cast had been taking their bows. He and Annie walked downstage centre and the applause grew louder. Everyone joined hands and the cast took a bow together. Arthur was holding Tony's other hand. As they lowered their heads, Tony heard him whisper, 'Well done, old boy.'

As soon as the curtain came down, everyone except Annie and Tony fled off stage for the dressing-rooms. He and Annie strolled into the wings, their arms around each other, still glowing from the last scene. Tony's mother was holding the door open for them and beaming.

Out in the corridor, Graham and Arthur dashed past them, their coats under their arms.

'Half a lager?' shouted Graham to Annie. 'Or a pint?'

'A pint please. I could drink a river.'

'G'night Tony. See you on Tuesday. G'night Jane,' he added, waving to Tony's mother. 'Have a good weekend.'

Annie ran up the stairs, Tony and his mother following on slowly.

Tony glanced aside at her, at the soft fine lines round her eyes that deepened when she smiled. Annie was right. She was a good chaperone. She didn't crowd him. Even when he got ratty with nerves, she just let it wash over her as if she understood.

'Mum, were you nervous about taking the chaperone job?'

'Terrified. I'd never met professional actors before, let alone worked in a proper theatre.'

'Like me, eh?'

'Yes.'

He slipped his arm round her waist.

'Was I really good tonight? See, I couldn't tell.'

'Not bad.' She smiled.

They stopped outside the dressing-room door.

'How about me then?' she said. 'Was I a good chaperone?'

He grinned and strolled nonchalantly into the dressing-room.

'Not bad.'

Sorry!

16 June 2001

Dear David,

I've tried to begin this letter so many times but I don't know where to start. This is my tenth attempt. So. Here goes! Again.

Firstly, I knew Dad had a cousin up north (your mum) and that she had a son (you). I remember you vaguely from five years ago when we met at my mother's funeral and I've thought about you loads of times over the years. Since you and your mum are our only relatives, I kept asking Dad why we never contacted one another. And he kept saying he would, but he is the procrastinator of all time and after my mother's death he was just too busy looking after me to do anything about it. So, when he received the letter from your parents saying they wanted us two to meet, I was so shocked.

Secondly, I'm sorry this is a letter and we can't phone or email one another. Dad found it difficult to join the 20th century let alone the 21st. For example, when a man from the phone company came ages ago and attempted to remove the old phone and replace it with a new one so that he could reconnect us, Dad refused to let him. He told him it was a perfectly good phone (and it is for an old movie), and that it's got plenty of life in it yet.

The phone company tried to persuade him to have a new reproduction phone. 'What do I want with a new reproduction phone,' said Dad, 'when I have the real thing?'

So you can imagine what he's like about computers. The nearest thing to a computer I can hope for is a morse code machine he's picked up at an auction.

Thirdly, I've enclosed a recent photo. As you can see, I have a round face, long straw-coloured hair and blue-green eyes. I've had it cut short since this photo was taken. My father did it to save money. It wasn't supposed to be short but he discovered that one side was shorter than the other so decided to even it up. You can guess the rest. Please send me a photo of you.

Yours, nosily,
Anna
(Your second cousin, or is it first cousin once removed?)

20 June 2001
Dear Anna,
I'm in shock too! Thanks for the photo. As you can see from mine, I have a round face as well. I'm on the 'plump' side. It's supposed to be puppy fat but I think I spend too

much time sitting and doing schoolwork.

Letter writing is fine by me. I have more privacy that way. If I emailed you a letter, I guarantee my mum would be standing behind me correcting it and polishing the computer at the same time.

I think my parents have contacted you because of the big five-oh (my mother's 50th birthday). She started talking about all the things she's been wanting to do for years and has never made time for, and going on about life slipping through her fingers and all that.

Mum says you're like me. Is that right? At my school the girls and boys hardly ever mix. Do you have cool cliques and uncool cliques? I'm so uncool, I don't even belong to an uncool clique.

Your new-found something-or-other cousin,
David

25 June 2001

Dear David,

Hurray for your mother's big five-oh! I couldn't believe it when my father read her latest letter. She's really determined we should get to know one another, isn't she? A whole fortnight here after you've broken up. They're very brave. And I'm not joking.

And yes, we have cliques at my school too. And no, I'm not cool. Nearly all my clothes are second-hand. Hey, I could start a second-hand clique! On second thoughts . . . or should I say second-hand thoughts (GROAN!).

But seriously, has Dad warned your parents about our place? Most people scream for a sedative after only five minutes here. But a fortnight? Let me explain. I expect they're looking forward to a holiday by the sea and it's true we live in an enormous house, a quarter of an hour's walk from it, but it's on a main road. If they don't mind the sound of traffic (worse in summer because you need the windows open), then that's OK, otherwise they'd better bring earplugs with them.

Now to the rooms. There are twelve of them if you count the bathroom and two loos. Most of them are very big and piled high with junk from auctions, including the hallway.

In the sitting-room, it's like an obstacle course getting to our televisions. We have twenty-one altogether. We use two of them, one on top of the other, because one gets a picture and one gets sound. To prepare you, let me tell you a little story which should give you a clearer picture of how normal people see us.

Three months ago, a retired couple from Yorkshire called Mr and Mrs Burkiss moved in a few doors along. Dad, being a Yorkshireman, decided to go and say hello so that they wouldn't feel lonely down South. I went with him.

They are both in their sixties, tall with white hair. You should have seen their place! Fitted carpets, new furniture, central heating, skirting-boards you could actually see and tea in matching cups. They gave us huge pieces of cake and were really friendly.

'Remember,' said my dad to them after tea, 'we only live a few doors away so feel free to pop in.'

'Do you live anywhere near that derelict-looking house, with the plank coming out of the basement window?' asked Mr Burkiss. (I forgot to tell you we have a huge basement as well.)

'No,' said my dad. I was amazed. My father lying? 'No,' he said. 'We live in it.'

They haven't been to see us.

I've left my pièce de résistance till last. The bathroom.

The bath is very old. It has lots of stains which won't come out, and claw feet. We used to have an enormous gas heater which made exploding sounds every time you switched on the water, but that's been removed and now we have an old immersion heater, which sits on the opposite wall. But Dad hasn't got round to filling in the holes above the taps yet. Talking of which . . . .

They are old, too. The hot tap (which the cold water comes out of), has had a cork stuck up its spout for four years. To get cold water into the bath we pull the end of the inner tube of a bicycle wheel up the spout of the cold tap in the basin and drape it over the bath. The cold tap in the bath (which the hot water comes out of), always rushes in a gush at first but within seconds it turns into a slow drip, drip, drip. It takes so long to run a bath that you can go to the newsagents two roads away to buy a comic and by the time you return it's nearly ready. Still want to come?

Yours, hopefully,
Anna

28 June 2001

Dear Anna,

You bet I want to come! Your home sounds like paradise to me. I can't believe your dad is my mother's cousin. We don't have any junk. I wish we did. I draw comic strips and I sometimes have several stories going at the same time or prototype drawings of the characters, and I daren't leave them or my Doctor Who comics lying around because by the time I've come home from school they will have disappeared, i.e. my mother has chucked them out.

And she's so tidy! I know where she hides the toothbrushes now but last night I spent fifteen minutes looking for the soap in the bathroom. In the end, I took up a new bar from the kitchen cupboard and she went up the wall because it was blue and that was the week for lemon towels. Lemon towels, lemon soap, you see?

In fact, our place sounds a bit like your Mr and Mrs Burkiss's. Sorry. So I've decided to hide your letter under the floorboards where I conceal the comic strips and cartoons I've drawn.

Got to stop now. Sorry. I have to finish hoovering my room because I forgot to hoover under the bed, inside the wardrobe and along the skirting-boards. I didn't exactly forget. I just hoped she wouldn't notice. If we had a cat, I'm sure I'd have to hoover that too.

Yours, overworked and hard done by,
David

P.S. I've had a horrible thought. Sorry! But supposing my mother starts cleaning your father's house? Usually when we're on holiday we have to do that before we go out. Every morning.

5 July 2001
Dear David,
There's no chance your mother will spring-clean our house. You'd need two skips and a dredger for each room, that's after you've used a bulldozer.

I'd love to live in a tidy house and have co-ordinating anything. I couldn't believe it when you told me about the soap. I bet it's scented too. My dad buys whatever he can get wholesale or down the market, so we usually have a box of fifty in vibrant pink or orange that smell of absolutely nothing.

How come your mother wants to stay with us? Perhaps she doesn't know my dad's deteriorated.

Yours, bewildered,
Anna

10 July 2001

Dear Anna,

She wants to, because as well as being an opportunity for us to 'bond' should our parents all die at the same time, and all we have left is each other (this is what the big five-oh does to you), it's also because my parents can't afford to go anywhere else for a holiday. Sorry. They've been saving every penny they can from both their wages to send me to a private school next term.

All my friends are going to the local Comprehensive, though come to think of it, I don't have any friends left now. I had to do so much work for the tutor on top of schoolwork, I never had any free time to see them.

Must stop. My torch has started to flicker. I'm sitting in the wardrobe hiding from my mother. If she catches me reading and writing and it's not 'school' work she says, 'Well, David, since you aren't doing anything you can go and hoover the garden.'

Lopsidedly, because I can't see anything now. (Sorry!)
David

13 July 2001

Dear David,

Poor you! I can't get into any of the wardrobes here to sit in and write because they're packed with stuff that might come in useful one day. Your letter reminded me to remind my dad that he'd better empty one before your parents arrive. Only two weeks to go. Yippee! You're having the room opposite mine on the top landing. Your parents will be sleeping two landings down so we'll be miles away from them. It's great at the top of the house, all sloping roofs, and there's a skylight on the landing. If you climb up and open it, you can see two bits of roof sloping into one another. And the sky of course.

Yours, full of plans,
Anna

P.S. Because you're coming and I pointed out it might rain for a fortnight, Dad has sold some stuff at an auction and brought home a second-hand television and video machine and they actually work! I have watched this really funny film called Some Like It Hot. It's about two musicians (men) who are fleeing from a gang who are out to kill them, so they disguise themselves as women and join a female band. Have you ever heard your dad talk about Marilyn Monroe? She's in it. She's one of the women in the band. You must see it when you come.

P.P.S. Can you swim? And if so, do you like it? Hope so.

P.P.P.S. Is there anything you can't stand eating?

15 July 2001

Dear Anna,

Brussels sprouts. Most vegetables really. Except potatoes and chips and raw carrots. And cucumber. Sometimes. But I like pasta. All shapes with melted cheese. But I'd better warn you, I'm a freak. I don't like hamburgers! Sorry.

I also like milk shakes. Chocolate is my favourite. And pizzas.

I hate meals which are what Dad calls 'meat and two veg'. It worries Mum sick.

Oh and I eat apples. Crisp green ones.

Will I drive your dad mad?

Yours, apologetically,
David

18 July 2001

Dear David,

My dad is the Pasta King! I hate brussels sprouts too. And guess what? I hate hamburgers! I was beginning to think I was the only person in the universe who did.

When you come to stay, will you draw some of your cartoons here? I can't draw very well but I like looking at other people's drawings. Do you know the Gary Larson Far Side cartoons? I read them on cards and Dad has been looking out for second-hand copies of his books. Last Christmas, they had loads of his books for sale in bookshops and I used to drag Dad in there and send him off to browse so I could read the cartoons. The bookshops here won't let children in unless they're with an adult.

The only books Dad buys new are the latest law books. (He's a lecturer in law at the new university.) And I've never seen a Gary Larson book in a second-hand bookshop. So that's the only way I can read them.

My other passion is trampolining. They have trampolines down at the sea front. Dad says he'll pay for us to go if you're interested.

Not long to go now.
Anna

21 July 2001
Dear Anna,

I have five Gary Larson books and I read them over and over again. I'll bring them plus some other cartoon books.

I haven't done much trampolining. I'd like to have a go, if you don't mind being seen with someone who will be falling all over the place. I've got two left feet. Sorry!

And I'll bring some videos in case it rains. I like the James Bond films except for the lovey dovey stuff. I cover my face as soon as I suspect he's going to kiss someone.

And I like science fiction. **Star Wars, Star Trek, Doctor Who, War of the Worlds.** I've recorded this film called **The Blob** where everyone keeps being chased by this thing which looks like a huge jelly and getting swallowed up by it. And it oozes its way through the ventilation grill into the projector room of a cinema and then through a tiny window into the auditorium. And all these people who've been watching the film run out of the doors screaming their heads off and it chases them down the street. It's scary and funny.

I've never seen Some Like it Hot. So let's do a swop.

Ahhhhhhhh! What's that behind me? It's horrible! Could it be the Blob? Could it be James Bond kissing someone? Could it be an invasion of Daleks? No, it's far, far worse. It's the sound of a hoover coming up the stairs!

Must go. Have lots of tidying up to do. Sorry!

David

25 July 2001

Dear David,

I can't believe it! Gary Larson and The Blob! I haven't seen it but it sounds brilliant!

So pleased you're into science fiction. There's a Star Trek exhibition down by the harbour this summer, with costume displays and film clips and everything! Dad says he'll take us, which is amazing, because he's usually so busy even after the university has broken up that we only talk about what we're going to do but never get round to doing it. But because you're coming, I think he'll be having a bit of a holiday too.

Only a few days now!

Anna

29 July 2001

Dear Anna,

Great!!!!! My dad wants to take us onto some old boats too and Mum wants to take some ferry trips. Can't wait.

We're spring-cleaning before we go.

Have packed cartoon books and videos and **Horrible Histories**. Have you read any of them? They're gruesomely funny.

See you soon,
David

14 August 2001

Dear David,

I miss you already! No one to go swimming with, no one to chat to in the middle of the night, and no one to crack Blob jokes with.

Guess what? We're off to the Isle of Wight for a fortnight's holiday! Dad is actually taking us on a proper holiday! It'll be the first time for five years. I'll send you a postcard saying 'Wish you were here' and it'll be true.

Yours, hoping there are no auctions on the island,
Anna

P.S. I hope you're remembering to give yourself a 5p forfeit every time you say 'Sorry!'

The high life.

Not a stove in sight.

20 August 2001

Dear Anna,

I couldn't wait till you got back to write. We've had fantastic news. I've won a scholarship! The letter had been delivered next door by mistake months ago but Mr Hodges had put it in his tool shed and forgotten about it, which is odd really since he works in the same office as Dad.

My mother still looks shell-shocked from our holiday with you. Sorry! Oh no. Sorry. Whoops, I'll start again.

She sits in our bathroom and gazes at it as if it's some magnificent painting. In fact, she's been doing a lot of silent gazing ever since we returned. I expect she'll come to by Friday though. I'm getting kitted out with my new uniform. Yuk!

I miss you chasing me with that red beanbag on your head pretending to be The Blob. I'll try and keep swimming but we live quite a way from the nearest swimming pool. Am also looking for a trampoline, but no luck yet. But I don't have to wear pyjamas anymore! Now I wear one of Dad's T-shirts, like you do.

Yours, a bit lonely,
David

P.S. I owe 10p from this letter. I still find it difficult to stop saying sorry. Sor . . . Whoops! Is that 3p?

3 September 2001

Dear David,

Congratulations on your getting a scholarship! Dad says congratulations too.

The holiday turned out to be great, although I thought we'd sink the car ferry on the way home. Our boot and roof rack were loaded with even more junk.

But your staying with us has got Dad and I talking about all sorts of things we've never got round to before.

He told me what he was like when he was your age. I don't know if you know this, but he came from a very poor background, which is why he's always looking for bargains and keeps going to auctions.

The problem with auctions is that things often get sold in lots, which means that if you get a really cheap toaster you have to take lots of other things with it, which is how we ended up with the seven pairs of crutches you saw on top of all the other stuff in our hallway.

He studied his way to where he is now, but though he's earning more now he still doesn't like buying anything new. One day on the Isle of Wight, he suddenly said to me, 'I don't know if I'm mean or just scared of being poor again.'

Also, most of his money gets swallowed up by our enormous house and we can't have anyone renting a room in it because the rooms are in such a horrible state.

He and Mum were going to do it up together. Dad said she was the more practical one and that she had great ideas.

And that was the most incredible thing about the holiday. We talked about Mum. Lots. I think Dad's been filling the house and his life with so much stuff, as a way of filling the empty space inside him after Mum dying.

He told me he covered up how upset he was after her death, because I was only six years old and he had to be strong for me.

One night we were walking along this deserted beach talking about her and suddenly we both started crying and we just held on to each other till we stopped.

When we returned to the caravan park, it felt like we'd let go of her and released her spirit into the sea.

The next morning Dad looked different. Younger.

Then we came home. To a wet awakening.

The first thing we noticed on the concrete drive were these gigantic puddles.

As we drove through them, the next-door neighbour called out to us over the wall. She must have been lying in wait.

'You've just missed the fire brigade,' she announced.

'Oh,' said Dad. 'Has there been a fire?'

'No,' she said, 'a flood.'

Someone must have put the plug in the bath (not guilty), and after a fortnight of the tap dripping, the bath overflowed through to the porch below and out under the front door to the street.

In the afternoon, a policeman came round and told Dad off because the firemen had found it so easy to break in, and hadn't he heard of Crime Prevention? (which was a bit embarrassing with all Dad's heavy law books on the shelves).

Back to the bathroom. The sink has sunk to one side into the hole in the floor beside it. It makes me feel like I'm at sea whenever I clean my teeth. If you lie down and peep through the hole you can see the porch.

Yours, not pleased,

Anna

18 October 2001

Dear Anna,

Sorry I haven't written. I have loads of homework every night, have to go to school on Saturday mornings, and then do weekend homework on Sunday.

I haven't made any friends yet and I still keep apologising. More now since I started my new school. I didn't know I did it so much before you pointed it out to me. Sorry! See what I mean?

I wish I could tell you that my mother has recovered from her holiday with you but I'd be lying. Dad had a good time though.

Dad has been playing the George Melly Sings Fats Waller LP your dad gave him and he and Mum unearthed all these old jazz cassettes and Beatles records from the loft, which I didn't even know were there. And Dad has started looking on the Internet for local jazz festivals! And I've discovered I like the Beatles!

I know he'd like to stay with your dad again. Only snag is,

if the bathroom is even worse my mother would be overdosing on Rescue Remedy (Dad says that's the herbal equivalent of tranquillisers). I really want to have a holiday with you again. It would give me something to look forward to.

We finally got around to watching **Some Like it Hot** and it even made Mum laugh! Wish you'd been there.

Yours, still lonely,
David

22 October 2001

Dear David,

Good to hear from you at last! I've had loads of homework too. But I've been luckier than you apart from that. I've made two new friends, a girl from my old junior school and a girl who lives only ten minutes walk away. That's the good news.

The bad news is that the girl from my old school travels from the Isle of Wight (her mum's in hospital so she's staying with her grandparents there). And the girl who lives near me is in a children's home and you almost have to have a letter from the Queen for her to come out during the weekend.

The good news. I asked Dad about the Beatles after your letter and he found this LP called **Abbey Road** and I can't stop playing it! It's brilliant! I've had some odd looks at school when I've mentioned it. But I don't care. Dad says it's nice to hear music in the house again, even though he was a Rolling Stones man.

'So how come you have a Beatles record?' I asked him.

It was Mum's.

The bad news. The bathroom is just the same. I'm working on it but I think it's a LOST CAUSE.

The good news. Dad has started clearing the house!

He contacted the Head of Drama at the University and asked if his students had ever thought of creating a play in which seven characters on crutches, who belong to a support group for people who have broken a leg while on a skiing holiday, share their experiences of how this has changed their lives. Dad said he was convinced it would make a very dramatic and emotional piece. And if he (the Head of Drama), was inspired, Dad could provide him with the necessary props. And then he started going on about post-traumatic piste syndrome or something.

We were in a call box at the time and I swear the queue outside could hear the Head of Drama laughing down the receiver.

Anyway, to cut a long story short, he's coming round to our house to look into our junk-filled rooms and Dad has said that if there's anything he'd like for his students, he can have it, providing he takes it away himself.

Yours, amazed,

Anna

10 November 2001

Dear Anna,

More bad news. My mother has persuaded my father to use the savings they would have used for my school fees on a swimming pool so that we can have holidays at home. We dig it and then a swimming pool firm will deliver bits of wall to slot in as we go along to stop the earth caving in.

Mr Hodges, our next-door neighbour, and my dad are going to dig it together. Since my parents will be giving up their garden for the pool, Mr and Mrs Hodges have suggested that they take down the fence between us so that we can share their garden and they can share our pool. It's all agreed. So it doesn't look as though we'll be having another holiday with you this year. Sorry!

Yours, gloomily,
David

P.S. Glad you've made friends. I haven't yet. The girls don't want to know me because I'm not 'cool' and the boys are into sports and skateboarding. Which holds no interest for me whatsoever. And most of their parents are really rich. I'm into history. Not cool. We're looking at the First World War at the moment. And it's making me so angry! The way the armchair generals sent thousands of soldiers to their deaths simply by using them as decoys. Massacre after massacre after massacre. I hate war.

14 November 2001

Dear David,

Oh no! They can't do this to us. Can't you sneak out at night and keep filling it up with earth?

Yours, in a hurry,
Anna

P.S. I hate war too.
P.P.S. You've made one friend. Remember?

1 December 2001

Dear Anna,

Good news. Mr Hodges wants to wait till after Christmas before continuing work on the pool. With any luck, he'll go on putting it off till next Christmas. Can't write any more. Homework to do. Masses of it.

David

Boxing Day

Dear Uncle Robert and Auntie June,

Thank you very much for sending us the lovely green bath mat. It will make getting out of the bath so much nicer. And thank you for the CD of Beatles hits!

Love Anna and Richard (Dad)

Boxing Day
Dear David,

I gave Dad a brand new tube for the cold water tap. It's six feet long. He was really pleased with it. I was amazed. He doesn't usually like new things, but he's not even going to wait until the inner tube wears out. He's going to use it today.

You'll never believe what my father gave me! A portable CD and cassette player with radio!!

He must have told your parents because when I opened their parcel with the CD in it, I had to hide the fact that I was disappointed that I wouldn't have anything to play it on. All I could say was, 'It's got a nice cover.'

So you can imagine what I was like when I opened his present. Good job we've got high ceilings!

About the bath mat your parents sent. He's put it away until we wear out the holey old towel we've got on our ancient lino.

And thanks for the towelling socks. It's been so cold I'm thinking of wearing them in the bath.

Yours, freezing,
Anna

2 January 2002
Dear Anna,

Thanks for the snorkel and flippers. When I opened them I said, in a loud voice, 'Oh good, I can wear these when I swim in the sea next summer.' My mother stared at me and said,

'Please don't mention the sea. It has nasty connotations.' Dad and I gave each other a miserable look.

I've hidden them under the floorboards. I don't have to tell you why.

But it's not all doom and gloom. My parents gave me a saxophone! And they've got a teacher set up and everything. It was when we were watching Some Like it Hot and I just said without thinking, 'I would love to play a saxophone.' But it wasn't a hint because I thought it would cost too much. And I forgot about it. But they didn't. I don't know how they kept it quiet for so long. Isn't it great?

Yours, and all that jazz,
David

2 January 2002

Dear Uncle Richard,

Thank you for the fine-tipped pens and the case for my saxophone. I suspect you knew what my parents were up to. And no, I don't mind that it's not new (the old one was falling apart). It makes me look like I'm an old hand, if you see what I mean. Like I've just arrived from New Orleans for my hundredth gig. When my granny saw it she said, 'Cool.'

Yours, saving up for shades,
David

16 January 2002

Dear David,

Too cold to write.

This morning, the washing on the line was so stiff Dad and I could prop the shirt and trousers against chairs. Dad said I wasn't to try and bend them in case they snapped.

The only consolation is that Dad chopped up a hideous wardrobe and a broken dressing-table so we could have roaring wood fires.

Yours, communing with icebergs,
when I'm not in the sitting-room,
Anna

18 January 2002

Dear Anna,

I'm disturbing Mr and Mrs Hodges with my saxophone practice. My parents have tried to sort out a time when I can do it, but Mr and Mrs Hodges don't want me to touch it at weekends. They say they can't stand the sound of it. And Mum and Dad want to be good neighbours, especially as Mr Hodges and Dad are going to be constructing the pool together.

Yours, definitely not feeling like Mr Cool,
David

23 January 2002

Dear David,

If only you could come and stay here. You could play the saxophone as long as you liked. We only have neighbours joined to us on one side. Guess what? Dad took me to this show performed by children and they were all brilliant! It turns out they go to three classes on a Sunday (drama, singing and dance), all in the same place. Each class is an hour. When it's my birthday, I'm going to ask him if I can go to one of them.

Watch this space!

Anna

1 February 2002

Dear Anna,

Dad and Mr Hodges began the hole two days ago, i.e. Dad did. Mr Hodges went indoors to make tea and study the measurements.

But last night it snowed and the hole is completely full. More snow is forecast tomorrow.

Yours, gleefully,

David

7 February 2002

Dear David,

Our pipes have burst. Guess where?

I knew something was up when the uncorked bathroom tap stopped dripping and I found an icicle hanging from it.

I have to wear an overcoat while I wait for the bath to run. Really.

Anyway, the night before last, there was this terrific explosion. Some of the pipes have snapped so now we have no water.

When the ceiling in my bedroom collapsed, it was six months before Dad got round to doing anything about it. If I don't have a bath for six months, I'm going to lose my new friends.

Yours, grubbily,

Anna

P.S. Mr and Mrs Burkiss said I can have a bath in their bathroom which is warm and luxurious!

18 February 2002

Dear Anna,

I burnt your last letter – as soon as I had finished reading it. My mother *thought* your bathroom was already pretty horrendous. (The horror! The horror!) But a bathroom with no water! She'd emigrate. Sorry!

More bad news. The snow has melted and my father has

been digging again. He said the sight of a bigger hole will spur Mr Hodges on, when he comes to help over the weekends.

My mother stands at the back door with a plastic bag for Dad's clothes, before letting him back in. It's a wonder he doesn't get pneumonia standing there in his underpants and socks.

Yours, hole-watching,
David

P.S. I'd love to go six months without having a bath, or even six days! I told my mother the other night that there was this report in the news that children were having too many soapy baths and that it was causing eczema. And think of the benefits to my skin if I skipped a bath. She said, 'That argument doesn't hold water but this bath soon will.' And she turned on the taps.

4 March 2002
Dear David,
Good news!

After convincing Dad that no one will want to stay with us (meaning your parents), if we don't have any water, he's actually going to get it replumbed!

Yours, over the moon,
Anna

12 March 2002

Dear Anna,

Great!

Now for my news. Mr Hodges has suggested my parents hire a digger over a weekend. My father pointed out that they would also have to hire someone to drive the digger and that it would mean having to buy a cheaper pool, and he and my mother wouldn't be able to afford a pool with very strong walls and special water-cleaning system.

Mr Hodges said it would take weeks for them to dig it by hand. Then Dad asked Mr Hodges if he wanted to back out. 'Oh no,' said Mr Hodges, 'I agreed it would be fifty-fifty and I'm a man of my word.' So Dad's still digging.

Yours, losing the will to live,
David

20 March 2002

Dear David,

We have brand new pipes in the bathroom!

And the taps work! All of them!

Tell your mother!
Anna

2 April 2002

Dear Anna,

I told my mother about the taps, but she just said, 'Pity we won't be there to admire them.' Sorry.

Pool news.

Dad has managed to dig two feet deep but the hole is now full of water!

We have something called a high water table because there's a riverbed near us. Dad's got to dig a smaller hole at the side of the big one for a pump. Until the water's pumped out, he can't do any more digging.

Yours, leaping up and down with joy,

David

7 April 2002

Dear David,

Brilliant! Here it is not so brilliant. I knew it was too good to last.

Within a week, all the pipes started rumbling and yesterday, when I was lying in the bath, there was a scuttling noise above me. A piece of plaster from the corner of the ceiling fell, hit the taps, and bounced into the bath. Through the hole came a pigeon's foot.

I quickly wrapped a towel round me and climbed over the boxes on the stairs, yelling for my father. He was in the hall. 'Dad,' I said, dripping all over the floor, 'there are pigeons in the roof.' 'Are there?' he said, and then showed me hundreds of packets of pizzas he'd got as a special bargain in the freezer fair.

> Yours, pigeon-foot-watching,
> Anna

15 April 2002
Dear Anna,
Sorry about the pigeon foot. Again I have bad news and good news.

The bad news is that Dad has dug the little hole and our garden hose is now attached to the pump in it. The good news is that we still have water in the hole.

The bad news is that the swimming pool people say we have to pump it out faster and Dad has agreed.

The funny thing is that Mr Hodges has been looking very pleased.

Dad's bought overalls, which he hangs on a nail outside and he won't let my mother touch them!

> Yours, not holding out much hope,
> David

30 April 2002
Dear David,
My bathroom saga has now become my pigeons-in-the-bathroom saga.

This afternoon, I came home from school and found one flying into the walls. 'Dad,' I shouted, 'there's a pigeon in the bathroom!'

'I know,' he shouts back.

'You know?'

'Yes, I'm waiting for it to tire itself out. It'll be easier to pick up then.'

I know what Dad's waiting means. I once found the skeleton of a dead pigeon in the corner of one of the top rooms. Even the maggots had died.

I don't like birds. But what could I do? I had to pick it up.

At least Dad opened the skylight window for me so I could throw it out but I noticed a hole in the roof and I'm sure there are thousands of pigeons gathering underneath it.

I worry in case the whole ceiling collapses and, one night, I'll find myself sitting in a bath filled with hysterical drowning pigeons all flapping their wings and clambering on top of me as if I'm some kind of life-raft.

Yours, an unwilling ornithologist,

Anna

10 May 2002

Dear Anna,

I destroyed your last letter immediately. My mother can't stand birds.

I have more bad news. Sorry!

My father is still digging.

Mr Hodges can only help at weekends and, when he does, he has to keep dashing off for hours to get special gloves to stop him getting blisters.

My mother has joined in! She's building a mixture of a rockery and a bank a few feet away from the pool. She's wheeling barrow-loads of earth, dumping and shaping it and then planting seeds in it.

Yours, at an all-time low,
David

P.S. I can't even think of any ideas for cartoons. Got any?

15 May 2002
Dear David,

Plenty. Right here. Sometimes I feel I'm living in a cartoon.

I've got used to the pigeons now. Sort of.

Have you asked your parents if you can come and stay again? Or has Auntie June still not recovered? Hey! How about you and your father coming and your mother staying at home?

Yours, all problems solved,
Anna

18 May 2002

Dear Anna,

I did what you suggested. My mother still hasn't calmed down yet! She says she looks forward to having a holiday with Dad and didn't I want her around or something? I've really hurt her feelings. I've had to be extra nice and extra tidy to make it up to her.

Yours, in the doghouse,
David

23 May 2002

Dear David,

Now it's my turn to say sorry! I didn't know your mother would get that angry. Sorry again.

Now what? I really want someone to go to the beach with this year. Dad might not make the time to come with me if you don't come again. And, as I told you, one of my friends lives miles away and the other lives in Fort Knox. And it's so difficult trying to organise get-togethers without a phone. So I got round to asking about those Sunday classes I mentioned, and Dad is going to let me do the dance classes and, if I like it, he may let me join the drama classes too!

So who knows, I might make a friend there.

Now, you need to take a deep breath and be sitting down before reading the next bit. Ready? Here goes. We've got a leak somewhere in our bathroom! Drips keep falling through the floor and into the porch.

The other night, Mr Burkiss called. I couldn't go downstairs because I'd just got out of the bath. Dad took ages to answer the door because he was in the kitchen at the back. Meanwhile, I could see Mr Burkiss through the hole in the floor.

When Dad finally opened the door, Mr Burkiss said, 'There are drips coming from your ceiling, Mr Wood.'

'Are there?' said Dad and he offers him an old umbrella.

Yours, in despair,
Anna

31 May 2002
Dear Anna,
Hole getting deeper. Banks round garden getting higher. Mr Hodges has twisted his ankle, which means he's had to rest.

So I've started helping now.

There's something I haven't told you about our family. I thought maybe your dad would have let on but when he didn't, I didn't mention it in case I upset my parents. But because of what's happened this week, I feel it's OK to tell you now. The other night Mum was taking a shower, after working all day and most of the evening in the garden, and Dad and I were sitting on a mound of earth with a cool beer and a coke, and I told him how you and your dad had talked about your mother on holiday.

I hope you don't mind.

So I asked him how come we never talk about Sean?

Sean was my older brother. He died when he was four years old. A year before I was born.

And you'll never guess what I discovered? I won't go into all the medical stuff, but Dad told me that my mother believed that if she'd kept the house cleaner he might not have died. That it was partly her fault that he was ill. But Dad said Sean was allergic to all sorts of things and that he was lucky to have lived till he was four.

But now I understand why she's so mad about cleaning and why she put off visiting your home after your mother died. I suppose she was afraid I might catch something and she might lose me too.

Anyway, she's discovered I'm healthier being dirtier.

When she came out of the shower in Dad's big towelling robe, I gave her a hug. She looked surprised but pleased too. And Dad appeared and said, 'We've been talking about Sean.'

And my mother's face sort of crumpled. Dad poured her out a glass of wine and handed her a large box of tissues and that's when they took the photo albums out. We stayed up till three a.m. talking about him.

It was really good and really weird at the same time.

Yours, with new muscles and blistered hands,

David

P.S. I hope you don't think I've turned traitor now that I've started digging too. I still want to spend a fortnight with you this summer.

170

7 June 2002

Dear David,

I forgive you. Thanks for telling me about Sean. I mentioned it to Dad and he looked pleased that I knew. He wasn't going to mention it unless you did. After all, he would have been my cousin too.

I'm sorry to tell you the leak in the bathroom is much worse now and it's made another hole in the floor, i.e. the porch ceiling.

I can't see your mother ever visiting us again. If we're lucky we might see each other in five years. We'll be sixteen and have yellow pimples and the bath will probably have come through the floor completely by then.

Dad has tried to call the plumber but he's never in. Dad says that if we wait long enough, we could have our very own shower cubicle in the porch and isn't that what I've always wanted?

Yours, wet,
Anna

11 June 2002

Dear Anna,

I am writing this in my school lunch hour. We've just had half-term and I have spent eleven whole days digging from breakfast to bedtime! My parents asked their bosses if they could have one of their week's holidays to coincide with mine. They've never dared asked before. They were afraid of losing their jobs. But they were given it! No problem.

The boys at my school asked me where I was going for my holidays and what would I be doing?

I told them I'd be digging in my back garden.

I didn't even say sorry!

They think I'm dull except this boy called Angus who's weird. At least I thought he was weird till he turned up at my home with a spade the day after we broke up. So, now I've a friend!

He's incredibly tall and skinny, smiles a lot and never combs his hair, and his clothes look like an advert for an Oxfam shop. He makes me feel relaxed because he just says what he thinks and it makes me laugh. And he likes me! Ordinary me.

Last weekend, his parents, his two young sisters, and one brother turned up with even more spades and loads of food.

Anyway, the pool is dug, all the wall panels are in, the swimming pool people have okayed it and this sandy concrety sort of mixture called screed has just been laid down at the bottom to make it nice and smooth. We're just hoping it doesn't rain before we get the vinyl liner in. Once the swimming pool water is in, we can turn off the pump because the weight of it will stop the earth water from rising.

We've nearly done it!

David

P.S. I feel much better now I can talk about Sean with my parents. I know this sounds weird but I think I've been feeling a bit guilty for being alive when I knew my brother hadn't made it. Like I had to apologise for surviving!

Dad believes that everyone is allotted their own life span and that Sean was only meant to live on this planet for four years, and he and Mum gave him the best four years they possibly could and that they loved him to bits. And by the way, they love me to bits too.

P.P.S. I showed my mother my cartoons and my comic strip stories and she thinks they're brilliant! And she not only wants to frame some of the cartoons and put them on the wall, but she's let me have a work table in my room, which can be as messy as I like, as long as I keep stuff off the floor! Is this a miracle or is this a miracle?

15 June 2002
Dear David,
It's a miracle! There must be something in the strata-wotsit because I'm having a miracle too!

Remember the Yorkshire neighbours, Mr and Mrs Burkiss? They're having a completely new fitted bathroom and asked Dad if we would like the one they're getting rid of. They don't like the colour. Dad said yes, of course. And, wait for this!

Mr Burkiss is a retired plumber and he's offered to put it in for us. He says he can't wait to get stuck into some work. Retirement, he says, is killing him.

Please tell your mother!

Yours, in a dream,
Anna

P.S. My dad says you can buy some very good clothes in Oxfam, especially suits. The sweaters aren't bad either.

22 June 2002

Dear Anna,

Disaster! Or sabotage! I know not which but I have my suspicions. It didn't rain. It didn't have to. The pump mysteriously turned itself off one night and by the time we got up, the pool was filled with murky brown liquid. It took days to pump it all out again, and new screed had to be laid.

I asked my parents if Angus could stay over and if we could sleep out in my old tent to keep guard. Mr Hodges didn't want peg holes anywhere near his lawn so we had to squeeze it in between a bank and the edge of the pool.

Anyway, the vinyl lining is in now. It's bright sky-blue with a mosaic design on it. The boiler for heating the water is arriving sometime this week. Mr Hodges has offered to pop round in his lunch hour to organise its arrival.

Dad has agreed. He says it'll be nice for him to have his

moment of glory. The trouble with my father is that he's too trusting and kind-hearted for his own safety.

My mother has been in a really good mood even though she looks dead tired, so I told her about your new bathroom and about Mr Burkiss. She said, 'That'll be the day!'

Yours, almost able to swim in my own back garden,
David

1 July 2002
Dear David,
Today is the day!

We now have a matching bath, basin and even a loo in an interesting shade of tomato.

I can't believe it!

Yours, in a hurry, watching the bath fill up quickly
out of the corner of my eye, as I write this,
Anna

P.S. Did that last bit make sense?

4 July 2002
Dear Anna,
Great news about the bathroom! My news is not so great.

The boiler arrived. It's sitting at the bottom of the split pool liner. Mr Hodges directed the man who brought it on a trolley vaguely in the direction of the pool and left him to make an urgent phone call.

The trolley went out of control and careered at full speed towards the pool. When my parents came home from work and saw it, my mother burst into tears. My father just stared at it.

There's been no sign of Mr Hodges for days. Mrs Hodges said he wasn't feeling very well.

Yours, down in the dumps,
David

7 July 2002
Dear David,
So sorry about the pool!

In a rush,
Anna

P.S. Can't write more. Have stacks of homework to do.

11 July 2002
Dear Anna,
It's finished and is being filled with water this weekend!

The swimming pool people were very apologetic about the accident. They came with a crane to haul the boiler out and have replaced the liner.

176

Only snag was it had to be driven through the Hodges' garden but my mother has promised to replace any damaged plants. She's so different now. Do you know I've actually seen dust in the house! I didn't recognise it at first. I had to take samples, photograph it and then look it up in the Encyclopedia Britannica. I've even spotted traces of dust on the hoover.

Anyway, the swimming pool people have been very helpful and in a fortnight's time, after we've finished putting down paving stones around the pool, we're having a party. It'll be a sort of Grand Swimming Pool Opening. It'll just be us, the Hodges, and Angus and his family. I wish you could come. Any chance?

I think the Hodges are a bit annoyed that it isn't just them and us.

I'll wait till this weekend when the pool is full of water before taking a photo of it.

Yours, definitely cheered up,
David

P.S. I'm cooking supper tonight! My parents have been looking so tired that I said I'd feed them. They were amazed. So was I! I couldn't believe I suggested it. I'm doing jacket potatoes, peas and chicken pieces. Impressed?

18 July 2002

Dear David,

Yes, I am impressed. But we can't make it to the Grand Opening. Dad says he's got too much to do here. Because the bathroom is being sorted, Dad is thinking of taking in a lodger so he's doing loads more clearing out. A week after the Head of Drama came and took stuff away in a van, he wrote to my dad and told him that one of their new drama lecturers is looking for digs, preferably a large room they can decorate and furnish themselves! Someone called Sidney Pigeon! I laughed so much when Dad read the letter out, I nearly wet myself. I just saw this huge pigeon in my mind, in a tweed jacket and spectacles. Dad thinks he can't be as fuddy-duddy as I imagine because he's in the drama department, but he must be with a name like Sidney!

Dad has warned him about the house in a return letter but this Sidney has already had a description of the house from the Head of Drama and isn't frightened at all. He plans to move in at the end of August and do some decorating before the term starts.

Latest bathroom news. Mr Burkiss has filled in all the holes in the walls and ceiling and asked my father if he'd like him to help him paint the walls.

Dad said, 'Do you really think they need it?' and Mr Burkiss said, 'Yes.' So then Dad said, 'I'll see what paint we've got.'

We're using the bath mat as a sort of colour check as we

go along. I'm painting too. Mrs Burkiss has been popping round with cake and pots of tea and she heard me say, 'Pity we don't have some green towels.' And she said, 'Why don't we dye the ones you have?'

So that's what we're doing this afternoon!

Yours, about to have a posh co-ordinated bathroom,

Anna

25 July 2002

Dear Anna,

This is a photo of the pool. Doesn't it look luxurious! Admire the clear blue water. Take in the ecstatic smiles of my tanned parents toasting each other with Sainsbury's champagne. Note that the flowers my mother planted have actually popped up on the banks!

I'm asking you to do all this because that's what it did look like.

On Sunday afternoon, we swam in it. Except Mr Hodges who sat in a deckchair beside it.

Then, on the following Thursday, one of the women in Dad's office, who was supposed to be taking her husband to some big weekend function in Bristol, had a car accident and my father was asked if he and my mother could take their place.

Dad was amazed.

Mr Hodges told them not to worry about the water in the pool. He would keep an eye on it. When I said, 'And I'll keep an eye on Mr Hodges,' my parents said, 'You won't be staying with them. We'll drop you at your granny's.'

We returned early Sunday evening.

The weekend was brilliant.

It was still light and had been a sweltering day so we were all looking forward to a swim. The first thing I noticed when we opened the front door was a note from Angus lying on the mat.

DEAR DAVID,
POPPED ROUND TO CHECK THE CHEMICALS IN THE POOL BUT MR HODGES WOULDN'T LET ME IN. TOLD ME I HAD A CHEEK. THOUGHT I'D COME FOR A SWIM WHILE YOU WERE AWAY. SORRY.

ANGUS

As I was reading this, I heard a shriek. My mother appeared to be having a nervous breakdown. My father was staring at the water in the pool. It was the colour of the bath mat they sent you. Green. Algae had got in, because the chemicals in the pool hadn't been checked.

My father strode into their garden and yelled out for Mr Hodges till he and his wife appeared. Then they had this almighty row, with my mother sobbing in the background.

And then it twigged.

Mr Hodges was jealous of my father being chosen to go off for the weekend.

At first my father just listened silently until Mr Hodges went on about my father having everything handed to him on a silver spoon and that people like him didn't know the meaning of hard work.

My father held out his calloused hands and said quietly, 'Let's see your hands now, Mr Hodges.'

When we came down to breakfast, the Hodges had put back their fence. They're going round telling people that we're snooty and that they worked hard digging the pool for my father and now we won't even let them swim in it.

Now for the most brilliant and stupendous news of the year.

The swimming pool place has an insurance plan and they're going to sort everything out for us. It means emptying the pool, cleaning and refilling it.

Because of my mother's overwrought state, they've advised my parents to take their holiday now and it'll all be done by the time we get back.

And my parents have agreed! And guess where they're talking of going? Your place! And to think I wasted all that time months ago planning pool sabotage when I had my very own saboteur next door.

Yours, snorkel and flippers at the ready,

David

P.S. I think you might spot something different about me when we meet. And it's not the fact that I'm taller. (I am, by the way.) I just noticed it the other day. I've stopped saying

'Sorry!' all the time. And guess what? I'm not even going to apologise for it!!

29 July 2002
Dear David,
Yes! Yes! And Yes! again.

I've told Dad you're coming. Well, I yelled my head off actually.

He's so pleased that I've nearly persuaded him to buy swimming trunks. New ones.

Here's hoping.

>Yours, ecstatic being the understatement of the year!
>Anna

30 July 2002
Dear David,
It was great talking to you on our reconnected phone last night! And your mother sounded very relieved about the bathroom.

Can't wait for her to see it.

The new taps work and nothing rumbles or rattles. It's so quiet, apart from the pigeons cooing and moving about. OK, so it's a bit cramped, but you can sit on the loo and clean your teeth at the same time. Dad said some people would pay for a luxury like that.

The walls and towels are now green. The floor is stripped

and sealed and the bath mat she gave us is by the tomato bath. It looks brilliant.

Let's go to the beach every day. Even if it rains.

Yours, hunting for a swim-suit that fits,
Anna

P.S. Wouldn't it be good if you could come every year? Then perhaps I could persuade Dad to get hot water in the kitchen. Did I tell you we haven't any now?
P.P.S. Eat this letter.

4 August 2002
Dear Anna,
Letter eaten.

Yours, hoover in hand but bags packed,
David

5 August 2002
Dear David,
Sidney Pigeon is a woman!!!!!

She had arranged to meet Dad at the house by letter before we had our phone reconnected. She's about thirty. And she's beautiful. She walked into the hall, beamed at the house and beamed at Dad. And Dad beamed back at her. All they needed was a full orchestra playing stirring romantic music, but instead they got an escapee pigeon flying down the staircase in their direction. They ducked in unison, still smiling at one another and the pigeon knocked itself out on the stand-up piano that is now in the hall. Dad got it at the latest auction. A real bargain.

Yours, gobsmacked,

Anna

P.S. I told Dad your mum can't stand birds. He says if it's too much, Mr and Mrs Burkiss have offered to put your parents up in their spare bedroom, but they only have one spare room so you can still stay with us. Hurry up and get here. I've so much to tell you.

From: Anna Wood
To: David Finch
Date: 15/06/03 5.49 p.m.
Re: And I thought the pigeons were noisy!

Remember last year when we had the invasion of the pigeons?

Last night, Dad and Sidney finished painting the big room on the landing below my bedroom and they've put a seal on the wooden floor. Some drama students went up there this morning – Sidney is directing them in this play. They're going to rehearse it here every Saturday from now on. It's by a man called Ionesco (sounds like youneskoh). She says it's absurd. You can say that again. Everyone has to be on roller skates! The noise is deafening.

Mr Burkiss has just finished putting the radiators in, in part-exchange for using the piano here for his piano practice. He looked so chuffed when Sidney presented him with phone numbers of piano teachers. He thought he was too old to start.

Mrs Burkiss is 'babysitting' me tonight when Dad and Sidney go to the theatre. Dad says I'm still too young to be left on my own even though I'm twelve years, one week and three days. But Mrs Burkiss is good company so I don't mind. She and Mr Burkiss are like the grandparents I never had.

We're lucky having them for neighbours. I wish you could have nice ones too. I'll try not to scowl at the Hodges when we come up to stay.

Yours, sympathetically,
Love Anna

From: David Finch
To: Anna Wood
Date: 15/06/03 6.37 p.m.
Re: GOODBYE!!!!

Last night we did what we always do to cheer ourselves up when the Hodges get us down, i.e. watched *Some Like it Hot* with big bowls of lemon sorbet. It's usually that or *Airplane*.

And at breakfast this morning, Dad said we'd better look

out for some more funny films to help us through the summer so I was going to email you for some ideas when I got back from school. Mum and I stepped outside to get into the car and there was a SOLD sign outside the Hodges' house. We didn't even know it was up for sale! Mum had to stop and park the car on the way to school she was shaking so much, to calm down.

Anyway, when we arrived back this afternoon we saw this man and woman and two boys about six and nine years old standing outside the Hodges' house. When we told Dad, he goes marching out there and says, 'Excuse me, you aren't going to be our new neighbours, are you?' And they said 'Yes.' And that they had exchanged contracts yesterday and were so excited that they just wanted to look at the house again. We knew that the Hodges were away but we didn't know if they had said anything about us.

Anyway, my parents invited them in. My heart fell when I heard that the man was an ex-guardsman. I thought he'd be stiff upper lip and all that. And then he spotted my saxophone and looked alarmed, or so I thought. And I felt my heart nosedive.

Then he says he's starting up a swing band for young people. Jazz. And would I be interested? I explained that I had only been learning the saxophone for eighteen months. But yes, please.

So they ended up staying for the rest of this afternoon and the two boys swam in their underpants in the pool and my mum and the other woman were sitting by the rockery in fits of laughter over something. I did hear the word 'algae' come up so I think I can guess what they were talking about.

Meanwhile, Dad, this man, and me just talked jazz and played CDs.

Magic!

Mum says when you come and stay, we're going to have a small barbecue-type welcome party for them, though it feels like we've had one already. They will have moved in by then and the Hodges will have GONE!!! I said, couldn't we have a goodbye party to the Hodges as well?

Great! Eh?

Yours, no longer 'singin' the blues',

Love David

From: Anna Wood
To: David Finch
Date: 15/06/03 7.03 p.m.
Re: Welcome Party

Dad jumped up and down when I told him your news. He says he's dying to get barbecueing again and would love to offer his services at the party. He also says he's just seen a really nice second-hand barbecue set. In an auction.

At which point, Sidney and I gave each other a look. We will be keeping a very close eye on him.

Mrs Burkiss has just arrived with a tub of dark chocolate ice cream.

Bye!
Love Anna

P.S. Dad says have you ever seen any of the Marx brothers' films? And how about Wallace and Gromit?
P.P.S. Though you won't need them to get through summer now, will you?
P.P.P.S. Cool.